POINT OF NO RETURN

TURNING POINT SERIES, BOOK ONE

N.R. WALKER

BLURB

BOOK ONE IN THE TURNING POINT SERIES

Matthew Elliot is one of LA's best detectives. He's been labeled the golden boy of the Fab Four: a team of four detectives who've closed down drug-rings all over the city. He's smart, tough and exceptionally good at his job.

He's also a closeted gay man.

Enter Kira Takeo Franco, the new boxing coach at the gym. Matthew can't deny his immediate attraction to the man his fellow cops know as Frankie. But in allowing himself to fall in love with a man known to his colleagues, Matthew risks outing them both.

Matt and Kira work to keep their relationship and private lives hidden from Matt's very public life, fearing it would be detrimental to their careers.

But it's not the other cops who Matthew should be worried about finding out his deepest, darkest secret... it's the bad guys.

COPYRIGHT

Cover Artist: Reese Dante
Editor: Labyrinth Bound Press
Turning Point Series © 2012 N.R. Walker
Publisher: BlueHeart Press

Third Edition
July 2017

Warning

Intended for an 18+ audience only. This book contains material that maybe offensive to some and is intended for a mature, adult audience. It contains graphic language, explicit sexual content, and adult situations.

Trigger warnings: Violence, kidnapping, and torture. Reader discretion advised.

DEDICATION

To Barbara Moore... for everything.

POINT
OF NO
RETURN
N.R. Walker

CHAPTER ONE

THE FOUR OF us hit the gym like we always did after a stressful day and were met by a round of applause from the other cops who were there working out. The gym itself was a main-floor space with various fitness equipment, a service desk, and some rooms off the far wall for different classes. It smelled like sweat and dirty socks. I loved it.

On the wall facing the treadmills was a row of TV screens, usually showing repeats of different sports. But not tonight. The TV screens were tuned to the five o'clock news, and all the guys there were watching the four of us standing outside the West Street headquarters.

A reporter introduced the story. "*Breaking another link in one of LA's biggest drug chains, Croatian expat Pavao Tomic was taken down in what can only be described as a successful drug heist by police.*"

I waved them off, heading straight for the treadmills. I didn't need to watch it.

I'd been there.

"*Detective Elliott, it must be a relief after weeks of hard work to finally have this notorious drug supplier in custody.*"

"*Yes, it is,*" I heard myself answer diplomatically on-screen. "*The streets of LA are safer. The people of LA are better off with Tomic behind bars.*"

What I couldn't say on air was that the slimeball deserved everything he got. With no regard for human life, types like Pavao Tomic were best left to rot in jail.

Instead, all suited up out in front of HQ, the television version of me went on to say it wasn't just me who did all the work, like the press insinuated, but a team effort.

I didn't outrank the other three men on my team. I didn't do anything they didn't do, but that wasn't how the media portrayed it. To them, I was the leader of the media-dubbed "Fab Four"—one of four detectives in the Narcotics Division who had broken crime rings right across the city. My partner, Detective Mitch Seaton, and detective partners Kurt Webber and Tony Milic made up the rest of the team who had seen a record number of criminals behind bars.

"Yeah," Mitch snorted from the treadmill beside me. "The one-man show here did it all on his own."

I rolled my eyes before looking over at the other guys. "Any time either of you three idiots want to speak up when the cameras start rolling, be my guest."

Kurt laughed. "No freakin' way! I'd rather your ugly mug be all over the news than mine."

"The general public would too," Mitch joked. He reached over and tapped the side of my face. "This pretty-boy makes all us cops look good."

Tony laughed at me, and the three of them started talking crap just like the media did. But they gave up trying to goad me when they realized I wasn't going to bite. I tuned them out and tuned into the rhythm of my feet hitting the treadmill instead.

They'd settled in to running it out on the treadmills

with me when Kurt told us he couldn't stay long because he had dinner plans with his girlfriend, Rachel. "Workout first, then we hit the bar, just for a few. It's been a helluva week."

And so it had.

We'd spent months watching Tomic, waiting for the intel to pay off, nabbing him red-handed in a multi-million-dollar drug bust. It had paid off today. No one injured, no casualties, several million dollars' worth of cocaine, ice, and meth off the streets, and one more link in the crime chain behind bars.

So we did what we always did. The four of us hit the gym, then we hit the bar. They didn't drink much, and I drank even less, but we'd blow off steam in the gym then unwind in the bar, talking crap and having a laugh. It was a cops' gym and a cops' bar. I'd been a cop for ten of my twenty-eight years. Police work was all I knew.

The guys I worked with were like my family, like brothers. I knew almost everything about them, as they did with me.

Almost everything. There was one part of my life they knew nothing about.

When the other guys commented on me being the blond-haired, blue-eyed playboy of the police force, the one all the ladies wanted, I was reminded of exactly what it was they didn't know about me.

Because it wasn't the ladies I wanted at all.

That was what they didn't know about me. That was what I kept secret. Hidden. Private. Would the guys I worked with treat me differently if they knew I was gay? Maybe... probably...

I wasn't ashamed. I wasn't scared. I didn't flaunt being gay because I didn't want it to precede me. I wanted to be known for being a *good* cop, not a *gay* cop. But above all, I kept my sexuality to myself because it was no one else's goddamn business.

After twenty minutes on the treadmill, I jumped off, ready for my bag workout. Boxing was my thing. The gym had a sparring room—no ring, just mats and pads. It was mostly just a form of fitness and a little self-defense. The other guys on my team didn't bother with it. They'd watch me spar sometimes, and they'd tease and taunt me, but not one of them had the balls to spar with me.

I headed into the boxing room, and Chris, the owner of the gym, followed me. "Hey, Matt!" he called from the door. "There'll be a new trainer taking your session today."

"No worries," I replied. "Is Vinnie okay?"

"Yeah, yeah," Chris nodded. "Just a change in his work schedule, that's all." He looked over my shoulder and called some guy over. "Frankie, this here is Matthew Elliott. He's your five-thirty appointment. Matt, this is Frankie."

I looked at him then, my new boxing trainer. And I got stuck.

Jesus fucking Christ.

I did a double take, trying not to give myself away. But he was fucking beautiful. He had dark hair, dark skin, dark eyes. He was European, or Asian. Or both.

He smiled. Oh, fuck. His smile.

"Frankie's real name I can't pronounce," Chris went on to say with a laugh. "But he knows I'm an ex-cop and not overly bright, so he forgives me."

This Frankie guy extended his hand and introduced himself formally. "Kira Takeo Franco." I couldn't detect an accent, but his name rolled erotically off his tongue. I shook his hand, and our eyes met. It was like I couldn't look away. His stare deepened for just a second and his eyes flashed, as though he could tell I found him attractive. Then he smiled and said, "You're the guy on TV."

"The one and the same," Chris said. "Anyway," he continued to me with a smile, "I've seen Frankie in action and thought I'd come in and watch how he does with our best student."

Then the door behind me swung open, and Mitch, Kurt and Tony walked in.

I looked at my team standing in the door, all smiling, then back to Chris. "And what are they here for?"

Chris answered hesitantly. "Well, Frankie's pretty good. I might have told them it could be... entertaining."

I looked at the three smiling cops, my so-called partners. "And you guys have come in to watch me get my ass kicked?"

They nodded and laughed, and Mitch defended me... well, kind of. "I got twenty on ya," he said. He threw his thumb back at Kurt and Tony. "These two aren't so confident."

I rolled my eyes and smiled at them, then started strapping my hands. When I turned around and saw my sparring partner, I almost lost my breath. He was stretching out—his broad shoulders were barely concealed by his singlet top, revealing well-defined muscles and beautiful, olive skin. My dick twitched.

Goddamn it.

A hard-on in front of my team was the last thing I needed. I faced the wall, bounced on my toes, and shook it out, wishing like hell my old trainer, the very not-attractive Vinnie, was still my trainer.

"Okay, we'll start on the bag," Frankie said.

He held the punching bag still while I practiced jabs and sequences, and he grinned. His dark eyes were bright and smiling as he held the bag steady. Even though I knew he was staring straight at me, I deliberately didn't look at him and kept my eyes on the bag instead.

But then he called time and picked up hand pads. He stood ready, his covered hands up between us, waiting for me to aim practice jabs into the pads. And in front of our audience, we went through the motions. I jabbed, he deflected. But he smiled as though he was daring me.

It was as though his full lips, his almond-shaped eyes, that shiny black hair, and the dimple in his left cheek were goading me. Luring me.

And my dick twitched again.

Fuck.

"Okay, Frankie," Chris called out. "Show him what you got."

Slipping his hands out of the padded mitts and throwing them to the sidewall, Frankie turned to face me. I faced him front on, raising my hands to protect my chin as he did the same.

We danced around each other for a while offering a few jabs each, and I noticed him lifting his right foot just slightly so his heel left the mat, but not his toes.

He wasn't just a boxer. He was a kickboxer.

"Keep your foot down," I told him.

His eyebrows lifted and he smirked, making my dick twitch again. And then he jabbed me twice in the mouth.

The other guys cheered as I pulled back, resizing my opponent. "Keep your elbows in," he instructed. "And keep your hands up."

I stepped in quickly, throwing a sharp left. He dodged it easily and grinned again, but this time he chuckled. And I could feel myself getting hard.

We exchanged a few taps, skirting around each other. I

landed a few good shots, as did he. But I was distracted, and he landed some rib shots and a few face shots. Not that he hit me hard, just a gentle tap to prove he *could* really hit me if he wanted.

One thing I learned real quick—getting tapped in the face and jabbed in the ribs does little for hard-ons. The more he hit me, the less turned on I got.

And just so I didn't get a fully fledged hard-on, I let him win.

I lowered my hands, just a little, and I didn't move my feet.

"Oh, come on," Mitch yelled at me. "What the hell do you think you're doing, Elliott? You can fight better than that!"

I knew I could, and I thought this Frankie guy knew it too, because not long after that, he called it quits.

Kurt and Tony crowed their victory, and Chris proudly clapped his new trainer on the shoulder. Mitch scoffed at me. "Yeah, thanks, partner. You cost me twenty bucks! It's your damn round. So get your ass to the bar and get buyin'."

I nodded, unwrapping my hands. "Yeah, yeah," I mumbled with a laugh. "Meet you there in five." I didn't even watch them leave.

Because then it was just me and him.

"Are you okay?" he asked, pulling strapping tape off his hand. "You were holding back on me."

I thought he'd picked up on that. I ignored his question. I ignored his smile and I ignored the fact we were alone. "You do martial arts?"

He nodded and smiled. "Yeah."

"I could tell," I said. "The way you lift your foot. It's a defensive move for kickboxers."

I looked at him then, and he was staring at me.

Fuck.

"Good detective work, Detective," he said with a grin. "Now why did you hold back? You don't seem the type to be intimidated by a little martial arts."

I snorted out a laugh at the likelihood of that. "I'm not intimidated."

He smirked and stepped closer to me. His eyes were so goddamn piercing, so brown they were almost black. His jet-black hair was damp and messy, and his perfect lips were smiling, just a little, in a smug kinda smirk.

Right then, I wasn't the kind of cop who could hold his own. I was a deer caught in headlights, mesmerized by this man, how beautiful he was. How close he was...

His voice was quiet. "So if you're not intimidated, are you interested? Because you look at me like you could be interested. And I have to say, I wouldn't mind."

Jesus.

I took an automatic step back from him, breaking my dazed trance, and pulled roughly at the tape on my hands. I cleared my throat. "I um... I ca—I can't." I was fucking stammering. And breathing too hard. "I have to go. They're expecting me."

Like some shit-scared little boy, I all but bolted out the door and into the showers.

Fifteen minutes later, cold-showered and somewhat clear-headed, I walked into the bar certain of two things.

If I was going to stay in my very comfortable closet, I needed to avoid my new boxing trainer.

And I needed a fucking drink.

CHAPTER TWO

I NEVER DRANK. Well, correction... I *rarely* drank. Four, no, make that five... five drinks and I was feeling it.

The guys were looking at me funny.

I knew they were looking at me funny, but I was pretending I didn't notice. I was keeping mum about my run-in with Frankie... Frankie... That really fucking sexy Frankie. I groaned and shook my head.

A smug Tony asked, "Could the ever-elusive Matthew Elliott be having girl trouble?"

"Know what?" I pointed my beer at him. "Fuck you." I swigged my beer proudly.

Tony scoffed. "Oh, I think it might be."

"Yeah, come on," Kurt said too cheerfully. "First, you take a beating from the new trainer guy, then you hit the beer? Spill the details, Elliott."

I downed the last of my drink, and when I pushed off my stool, the room tilted. I tried to reach for the table, but it was somehow not as close as I thought. Then the room tilted again, and Mitch had hold of me.

Mitch. The best partner a cop could have. I told him this, of course, and he agreed.

"Get him home," someone said. Kurt. Kurt said that.

I told him, very seriously, "I can get myself home, thank you, Detective Webber."

Kurt and Tony laughed at me. They were *laughing at me*, and it should've bothered me. Actually, it did bother me, but Mitch was pushing me out the door.

Ah, Mitch. My partner. "Haven't you got a movie date tonight with Anna?" I asked.

He looked at his watch. "Plenty of time," he said. "It's not even eight."

Fuck. It wasn't even eight and I was smashed. The fresh air and city lights outside the bar seemed to make me drunker.

I looked at Mitch. "Whose idea was it to have beer?"

"Mine," he said with a snort. "But it was your idea to have bourbon."

Ugh. Bourbon. I hated bourbon.

"Oh, here's Frankie."

No. No, no more Frankie.

Mitch was mumbling about his jacket, and I turned around and was looking at dark, almond eyes and perfect lips. And then the sidewalk tilted.

Fuck.

"Here, hold him up," Mitch said. "I left my jacket inside."

Then big hands were on me. Strange hands, unfamiliar hands... Warm, strong hands.

I watched Mitch walk away and looked at this Frankie guy. "It's your fault," I told him. Because it *was* his fault.

"What's my fault?" he asked with a smile.

"That smile," I groaned. "It's too beautiful."

So he smiled again. Of course he did.

Didn't he know what he was doing to me when he smiled? Didn't he understand at all? "You'll give me away." I leaned in so I could whisper, "No one knows about me, okay? No one knows."

"No one knows what?" Mitch's voice came from behind me.

Spinning around to face him, I joked, "How fucking good I am."

"Yeah, right," Mitch laughed at me. "We all know how good you are." He looked over my shoulder to Frankie. "Hey, thanks, man."

"No worries," Frankie said, then his hands weren't on me anymore. "I just finished up at the gym and was heading to the parking lot," he explained. "You gonna be all right with him?"

"Yeah," Mitch chuckled close to my ear. "This is what three beers and two bourbons will do to someone who doesn't drink."

"Doesn't drink, huh?" Frankie asked, looking at me. His dark eyes were all glimmery, and he smiled that fucking beautiful smile. "Looks like he managed okay."

Mitch groaned like I was hard to hold onto or something. "It's been a big week, but something got under his skin today."

"Is that so?" Frankie asked. "And he's gonna be sick tomorrow."

They were talking about me like I wasn't even there. Well, fuck them. I just wanted go home. I patted down my pockets. "Where's my keys?"

Mitch laughed again. "You're not driving anywhere."

"I can drive just fine," I told him. Then I looked at the road. It looked wobbly. "If the road would just stay still."

Mitch put his arm around me, and we started to walk. "What about my car?" I asked.

He shook his head at me. "Your car can have a sleep-over," he answered. "I'll pick you up in the morning."

Ugh. The morning. I was gonna be sick in the morning.

Mitch mumbled, "I know you're gonna be sick in the morning."

Mmm. I must have said that out loud. I tried not to say anything, in case I said the wrong thing and drunkenly stumbled out of the closet. I'd never been so rattled by anyone before.

I looked around. "Where's that Frankie guy?"

"He left us on the sidewalk," Mitch said. "Jeez, how drunk are you?"

I had to think about that. "I'm pretty fucking drunk." Then I told him, "I let him beat me."

Mitch propped me up against a car, *his* car, and he looked at me. "I know you did. It cost me twenty bucks."

I opened my mouth to speak, but then I remembered that I was trying not to talk in case I said too much. "Ssh, it's a secret," I told him, locking my lips and throwing away the key.

"You gonna tell me why you let him beat you?"

I shook my head and pressed my lips together. "Mm-mm."

He laughed at me again, shook his head, and stuffed me into his car. When we got to my place, he hauled me up the front steps, bitching the whole way, and when he finally got me inside, he threw me on the couch.

"My bed," I said, hearing myself slur. Fuck, I was drunk.

Mitch slapped my face. Twice. Then he grinned. "I don't love you that much."

"Fuck you," I said, though it sounded a bit mumbled.

"I'll be here at seven-thirty in the morning to get you," Mitch said. "You'd better be ready."

The last thing I remembered was hearing the click of my front door, and the only way I could stop the room from spinning was to close my eyes.

WHEN MITCH ARRIVED in the morning, I was dressed and ready for work. And very hungover.

He pulled the blinds, so the sun burned my retinas and made dust swirl around my sparsely furnished living room. I closed my eyes and held my head.

"You in the land of the living?" he asked too damn loudly, as he handed me a coffee.

"Barely."

He laughed at me, shaking his head. "Come on. We've got a mountain of paperwork to get through."

Ugh.

So with a thumping head and queasy stomach, I spent the next too many hours buried in paperwork.

"Oh, hell," Mitch said, distracting me from my thoughts. "You've got that look."

"What look?"

"That 'something's not right' look you get when you think we've missed something."

"What is it this time?" Kurt intervened, looking up from his desk.

I threw the file I was holding onto my desk and sighed. "He didn't work alone."

Mitch, Kurt, and Tony all groaned. They knew who I was talking about.

I tried my case again. "I'm telling you, he couldn't have done this on his own."

"We've been through this," Tony said. "There wasn't anyone else. Tomic acted alone."

Kurt's brow creased. "Matt, we checked this out. There was nothing."

I groaned. I knew. I knew we'd been through this. We'd checked it out, but something just didn't add up. Something was missing. I was rarely wrong on things like this, but I had no proof.

"Well, you've got about four months to prove it," Mitch said. "Hard, damning, physical evidence kind of proof."

Mitch got up from his chair and threw two case files on my desk and clapped his hands on my shoulders. "So while you're working on that, have some new cases with new bad guys to go over in your spare time," he said with a smirk.

"Mmm." I huffed, knowing any hope of constructive argument was over. Resigned, I closed the Tomic file for now and picked up a new case file.

New case. New bad guy. Report after report. It never fucking ended.

I found myself absorbed with intel on a new possible drug ring, and after a while, Mitch threw his pen onto his desk. Closing the folder in front of him, he looked at me. "It's five o'clock, Matt. Gym and bar?"

I shook my head and rubbed my stomach. "Not me. Not tonight."

"Oh, come on," he whined. "It's Friday. Not very often we get Friday nights off."

"I'm not up for it tonight," I told him.

Tony scoffed. "Not up for bourbon? Or not up for another ass-kicking from what's-his-name?"

Frankie. Fuck. I hadn't thought of him all day.

I laughed them off, but they weren't letting me out of it. Mitch grinned. "The workout will do you good."

"No beer, no bourbon," Kurt added with a laugh.

I groaned. It really would be less painful if I just went along with it.

"No boxing," Mitch said seriously. "I can't afford it."

No, neither can I. Considering I didn't have a boxing appointment, I should've been safely able to stay away from the new trainer. With a bit of luck, he wouldn't even be there.

I stood up. "Even hungover, I could kick your asses on the treadmill."

Mitch chuckled, grinning at me. "There he is! The smug, self-righteous son of a bitch we all love."

Twenty minutes later, we were at the gym. There was no sign of Frankie, and we were all back to good. We were running it out, laughing and joking. Kurt and Mitch both had something on with their girlfriends this weekend, and Tony had a dinner with his in-laws.

I laughed at them. "Glad to be single."

"Yeah, well," Kurt snorted. "When do we get to meet the girl who got you all bent out of shape last night?"

"What?"

"Oh, come on," Tony huffed. "To see you get your ass beat on the mats"—he gave a pointed nod to the boxing room—"and then get drunk? It's gotta be a woman."

I hit stop on my treadmill, slowing to a walk.

Fuck, fuck, fuck.

As part of the straight game I played with these guys, I just smiled at him and said nothing, letting them assume what they wanted.

I'd never lied outright to them. I'd never said *he* or *she*. I'd always kept it vague. They were the ones who assumed.

I jumped off the treadmill and wiped my face with my towel.

"Told ya," Tony puffed to the other two. "It's gotta be girl trouble. Playboy Matt Elliott's got himself a girlfriend."

I rolled my eyes at him and, needing to put an end to this conversation, walked into the boxing room. They laughed behind me, even louder when I flipped them off. Thankfully, the room was empty. I strapped my hands and spent a good twenty minutes punching the bag.

I could feel the sweat pouring out of me. The stress unknotted in my shoulders and last night's alcohol-induced funk did too.

I unloaded on the bag, having missed my usual workout bout because I was so distracted by the new trainer. I unleashed jab-punch combinations, relishing the feel of power, the de-stressing and the burn in my muscles.

"I knew you were holding back," a smooth voice said behind me.

I spun around, though I already knew who I'd find. Frankie grinned at me, and my chest tightened.

"You feel okay today?" he asked. "You were a little unsteady on your feet last night outside the bar."

Oh, fuck. I'd forgotten about that. I'd spoken to him... Shit. I ran my hands through my sweat-soaked hair. "Last night is a bit of a blur," I admitted. "I'm sorry if I said... anything," I finished quietly. "I don't normally drink."

He nodded. "You might have said something."

Ugh. I groaned.

"Don't worry," he said with a smile. "You made some things pretty clear."

I stared at him, trying to remember what I'd said. He pulled out some mats and pads, throwing them on the floor. "You told me no one knows," he said softly but seriously. He picked up my towel, walked over, and handed it to me. I was unable to move—frozen in place. Whispering, so only I could hear, he said, "And you think I have a beautiful smile."

It felt like the air had been sucked out of the room. Fuck. I made my legs move and took a step back from him. I could feel the blood draining from my face, and my heart was beating double time. I tried to tell him he was wrong. I wouldn't have said that. I wouldn't have let my guard down, no matter how beautiful I thought he was.

"Hey," he said softly with his hands up, palms forward. "No one knows. I get it. I won't tell anyone." His dark eyes were staring straight into mine. I knew enough about reading people to know he was telling me the truth.

"I wish I could say the same about your smile," he said almost wistfully, looking at me with those goddamn beautiful eyes. "But I've yet to see it. I'd *really* like to see you smile."

I tried to swallow, but I couldn't. My mouth was suddenly too dry. So I nodded instead.

The door swung open behind us, and it propelled my legs into motion. I stepped away from him, toward the door, where a woman stood.

"Ah," Frankie said behind me. "My six o'clock."

The girl, though I wasn't sure who she was, nodded and addressed me with a curt, "Detective Elliott."

I nodded back, then wiped the towel over my face as I walked toward the door.

"Matthew?"

I spun around at the sound of his voice saying my name.

He grinned at me. "Your next appointment with me is Monday. See you then."

I nodded, almost bolting out the door. Shit. My next

appointment... I had two, sometimes three boxing sessions a week. Which meant, if anything, I'd get to see him at least twice a week. The thought alone filled me with a little bit of dread. But I could feel something else settle into my stomach. Something I didn't want to admit... something that might have been anticipation.

CHAPTER THREE

I SPENT the weekend trying not to think about him. I even considered hitting the gym on Sunday so I didn't require my Monday appointment with him. But I wasn't one to run and hide. Surely I could face off with this guy, no matter how hot he was, without one, getting a hard-on, and two, being a gibbering idiot. He must think I could barely form a sentence.

I was a detective, for fuck's sake. A fucking good detective. I just needed to get my act together when I was around him.

I steeled my resolve, and my Monday appointment started out just fine. I hit the treadmill first, as always, and when I'd done my five miles and it was right on five-thirty—and when I couldn't put it off any longer—I walked into the boxing room.

He was in there warming up with a jump rope. His bronze-colored torso flexed fluidly under his loose tank top, and his feet barely hit the floor. He was agile for someone of his size. He wasn't huge, but he was tall with great muscle definition.

He smiled when I walked in and hung up the jump rope on one of the hooks on the back wall. I tried not to think about his smile or his body, and needing a distraction, I started to strap my hands.

Like he seemed to understand the effect he had on me, he was all business, though he still smiled. He was still fucking beautiful, but he wasted no time on putting me on the bag, only this time he didn't hold it so he wasn't facing me. Which was much better.

I found it easier to concentrate when I wasn't looking directly into his eyes.

He stood at my side and corrected my footing. Apparently my left foot turned in when I stood in position, making my right swing overcompensate.

By the time my half hour was up, he had improved my focus. I'd hardly had time to think about him. He was good at what he did, of that there was no doubt.

When I was done, he threw my towel at me. "That's better, Detective," he said with a one-dimpled smile.

He had a sheen of sweat over his shoulders, and his tank top barely covered him, his pecs, his shoulders. *God, I was in trouble.*

"Yeah, it was." I pretended to wipe my face with my towel to cover the fact I'd just checked him out.

"More focused today," he said.

I let out a nervous laugh. "Something like that."

When I looked up at him, he was staring at me. "Oh, I almost got a real smile," he said with a smirk.

I could feel myself blush. Fucking hell. I couldn't help but smile a little. "Almost."

"I think you should call me Kira," he said, matter-of-factly.

"Why?"

"Because it's my first name," he said with a shrug. "And everyone here calls me Frankie."

He must have seen the confusion on my face, because he clarified. "See, if you tell your friends at work you're having dinner with Frankie, they'll know it's me. But if you tell them you're having dinner with Kira, they won't have a clue."

"Are you always so forthright?"

"Yes."

"Why me?"

He barked out a laugh. "Have you seen yourself lately?" he asked. "And I'm intrigued by you."

"Oh" was about the most intelligent thing I could say.

"So, what about dinner?"

And right then, someone else—another cop—walked into the room, saving me from answering.

Kira smiled at his next appointment, and when I got to the door, he called out to me. "Matthew?"

I turned and waited for him to continue.

"Think about what I said," he said, straightening out the mats. "And I'll see you for your Wednesday appointment."

Fuck.

He'd basically just asked me to have dinner with him. He'd asked me to call him by his given name so the guys I worked with wouldn't catch on. It wasn't that I was really considering it—because a part of me was already looking forward to it.

But I didn't get to see him on Wednesday. I got caught up with work and missed my appointment. My job was hardly Monday to Friday, nine to five.

But he was all I thought about, his smile, his lips, his eyes... his offer.

And by Friday afternoon, after a long week, we headed

to the gym early. I did my usual time on the treadmill before heading into the boxing room. I wasn't even sure what I was going to tell him, whether I'd take him up on his offer or not. I wanted to... God, I wanted to. But I had my reservations— something I knew I should tell him about before this went any further. *If* it went any further.

When I walked into the room, he was with another appointment. "Oh, sorry," I mumbled. "Didn't realize you had someone else in here."

He smiled when he saw me. Looking to the clock then back to me, he said, "No, it's okay. We're nearly done. You can start on the rope for me, if you like?" he asked, nodding toward the jump ropes on the far wall. "We'll be another five minutes."

Throwing my towel and water bottle onto the mat in the corner, I picked up a rope and faced him as I started to skip and watched him with his appointment.

It was a woman. She was a cop on the fourth floor, I think. I'd seen her around. She was quite attractive, in a female kind of way—blonde, thin, and fit.

He had her, with her back to me, jabbing into the punching bag while he held it. He was facing me. Looking at me.

He still gave her instructions like "square your shoulders," "chin down," "move your feet."

But he was looking directly over her shoulder, straight at me, as I jumped rope. "Much better. Looking good," he said, almost smiling. His eyes were intense. Even though he was saying it to her, he wasn't really. He was saying it to me.

It made my dick throb.

So I turned and faced the mirrored wall, hoping it would distract me enough. But as I watched myself jump rope, I could see him in the reflection.

Even though I had my back to him, his gaze met mine in the mirror, and it somehow made it worse. He was watching me, inconspicuously, but still... I could feel his eyes on me, burning into my skin.

I watched him watch me, our eyes locked in the mirror, until the woman he was training said something, his eyes darted to her, and the connection between us was broken.

He wrapped up his appointment, so I hung up the rope and started strapping my hands, sure of one thing.

This appointment was going to kill me.

Needing to focus on the task at hand, I started on the bag while he talked to Jenny, Jane, Janette, whatever the fuck her name was. When she'd left, I knew he was standing behind me, just watching me, but he said nothing.

I knew we were alone in the room—my body seemed to know it. I stopped hitting the bag, held it steady, and rested my forehead on the bag, not realizing how hard I was breathing.

"What are you doing to me?" I heard myself ask, not really meaning to say the words out loud.

He cleared his throat, seemingly surprised by my words. "What do you mean?"

I looked at him then and figured maybe if I said this shit out loud, I'd get it out of my system. "You," I said, almost accusingly. "You're all I can think about."

He looked down to the floor mats. "You missed your Wednesday appointment. I thought maybe you were telling me you weren't interested."

So not only had he noticed I wasn't here on Wednesday, he had also missed me. I liked that more than I should've.

"I was working," I explained. "See, that's the thing with me and why this would never work. My job."

His brow pinched. "Is that a reason or an excuse?"

"Look, Frankie... Kira," I amended, and he almost smiled. "I'm a narcotics detective. I don't work set hours. My job is hard on relationships. Just ask any of the guys—their wives and girlfriends will tell you it's not easy."

He smiled shyly. "While I like the sound of a relationship, I thought maybe we could start with a casual dinner."

I barked out a laugh, a little embarrassed. He stood on the other side of the punching bag and held it between us. "But let me guess," he said. "You got burned once, maybe even had your heart broken, and you swore you'd never do it again."

I ignored that. "Kira, thanks for the offer—and believe me," I said, looking him up and down, "I'm very interested, but I'm also *not out*—no one at work knows." I tried to explain. "In fact, they all assume I'm some playboy with a different girl every weekend."

He looked right at me. "But you've had other dates? Other boyfriends?"

So I opted for the honest truth. I nodded. "Yeah, some. And it always ends the same." Then I quickly added, "I don't want to get involved only for you to turn around in a few months and leave." I finished quietly, "I don't expect anyone to step back inside the closet for me."

Kira huffed. "Well, thanks for not even giving me the chance. You know, I thought you said you were interested."

I sighed. I was interested. Too interested. "Believe me, I'm doing you a favor."

"I'm a big boy. I can look after myself," he said with a hurt, somewhat defensive smile.

"I'm sorry," I told him. "I wish it were different."

"Do you think this is easy for me?" he asked seriously. "You know, I saw you and thought you'd be someone I'd like to get to know. I don't make a habit of just asking random people out, especially guys at my work. No one here knows I like guys. Do you think they'd have hired me if they knew? In a *cops' gym?*"

I hadn't thought of that.

He walked into the middle of the room, turned, and looked at me. "I think I'll be the one to judge what's good for me." He held up his hand and curled his fingers, motioning me over to him. "Come on, put your hands up." He stood in the ready sparring position. "This time don't let me win."

I shook my head and exhaled loudly. Jesus, he wasn't letting me out of this. *Okay*, I told myself, *I can do this*. I walked over to him and mirrored his stance. With my hands up to protect my chin, I jabbed a few times with my left and landed a few with my right.

We sparred for a good five minutes or more. He gave me a few light taps to the face, and when I gave it back to him, he grinned at me. "Now, why couldn't you do this the first time we sparred?"

So I told him. "Because the only way for me to not get a hard-on around you was to let you hit me."

He laughed—really fucking loudly—and he dropped his hands. So I jabbed at him with my right, not expecting him to be so close, and my fist connected with his mouth.

"Oh, fuck!" he said, pulling back quickly, holding his hand to his mouth.

"Shit, I'm sorry," I said, but I also kind of laughed at the same time.

"Was that a diversionary tactic?" he asked.

I laughed again. "No, seriously. I mean, I meant what I said about the hard-on. But you shouldn't drop your hands."

"You shouldn't mention hard-ons."

I laughed again, and he chuckled. But he was still

holding his hand to his lip, so I told him, "Let me have a look at it." I pulled his hand away to inspect his lip. It was split, there was blood, but his teeth were still intact. I smiled at him. "You'll survive."

I grabbed his water bottle and threw it to him. And when I handed him his towel, he wiped his face, dabbing it to his lip.

"Am I still beautiful?" he asked with a smile. His tongue darted out to lick his swollen lip.

I looked at him, split lip and all, and nodded. "Yep."

He grinned then, making his lip bleed again. "Shit," he cursed, holding his towel back to his lip. "I don't know," he mumbled through the material. "I think this will cost you dinner."

I snorted, and he groaned. "Now, if you don't mind, I need to fill out an incident report," he said, holding up his towel to show me. "Blood spilled."

He walked out of the room, and I presumed our training session was over. Jeez, it was just a split lip.

I pulled the tape off my hands, collected my things, and walked out into the main room, where Kira was behind the counter writing in some book. Chris, the gym owner, smiled and shook his head at me. "What are you doing giving my staff a bloody lip?"

I shrugged. "He zigged. He should have zagged," I said, making Chris laugh.

Mitch jumped off the cross-trainer. He tried to catch his breath. "You couldn't have done that last week? When it cost me twenty bucks?"

I rolled my eyes at my partner. He was never gonna let me forget that. Ignoring Mitch, I walked over to the counter, where Kira was still writing. "Do you really have to fill out an incident report for a split lip?"

He grinned and handed me a slip of paper. "Something like that."

I opened the folded note to find it wasn't any kind of incident report. It was an address and phone number. And three words.

DINNER. *Eight o'clock.*

I FOLDED the piece of paper and couldn't help but smile. I hid it in my hand just as Mitch walked over. He was mumbling at me, something about it being my turn to buy at the bar. "Frankie," my partner said, "you should come to the bar with us. Elliott here owes you a drink for the fat lip."

Kira looked at me, then back to Mitch. His swollen lip curled into a smile. "Thanks. But it'll have to be another time, guys. I've got a date tonight."

CHAPTER FOUR

____

I PULLED up at Kira's apartment complex, still not sure what I was doing. It was a big enough building that if I was spotted parked here or even seen going inside, there was no way anyone could know who I was visiting. But I was still nervous. This was about to breach the rules I'd lived by for years.

But there was something about him, his dark eyes, his smile...

Whatever it was had me sitting in my car, all nervous about going inside. Part of me was thinking this was reckless. He was too close to the guys at work, the gym, my real life. If it ended badly, or if he was careless with a look, a touch, a comment, he could expose me. He could out me.

I was waiting for the rational part of my brain to tell me to keep driving and forget about him.

But he was just as vulnerable as I was. He wasn't out at work either. He was keeping the same secret.

It was so unlike me, but I was drawn to him the second I saw him. I'd never felt such an immediate attraction to anyone before like I had with him.

I wasn't quite sure what it was, but the next thing I knew, I was walking across the street into his apartment building and knocking on door 7F.

"Ah, hang on," his voice called from somewhere inside.

Bouncing on my toes, I briefly asked myself what the hell was I doing—when he opened the door. And he was standing there. Fuck.

Dark blue jeans, a white button-down shirt—and bare feet.

"You're early," he said.

I looked at my watch. 7:52 p.m. "You said eight?"

When I looked at him, he was smiling. That steal-my-breath, make-my-dick-twitch kind of smile. I exhaled slowly, and he stood back, silently inviting me inside.

There were shoes at the door, and given he was bare-foot, I took it he had a no-shoe policy. I quickly pulled off my shoes and left them by the door, and when I looked up at him, he was still smiling.

His eyes glimmered. "I wasn't sure if you'd turn up."

I nodded. "Neither was I."

He grinned at me. I was nervous, and he could tell. I took a deep breath and looked into his apartment, searching for a distraction. It was nice, not huge, but light, tastefully decorated and clean—and something smelled fantastic.

"Something smells great," I told him.

"Something's gonna burn," he said, walking into the kitchen. "I hope you like paella."

My stomach growled right on cue. "Um, yeah. I do, actually."

And when I followed him into the small kitchen, I could see the huge pan on the stove. "You cooked it?"

He stirred the pan and chuckled. "Sure did." He looked

at me, and again, I was struck by how close we were... how alone we were.

"Want a beer or wine?" he asked. "Or there's soda or water." He nodded pointedly toward the fridge, and I presumed I was to help myself.

There was an almost empty bottle of Sam's on the counter beside him, so I picked two from his fridge and handed him one. I figured the beer would relax me and give me something to do with my hands so my nerves didn't give me away.

But he seemed to pick up on my nervousness—either that, or I was just really obvious—because he started talking.

He talked about sports, his work, my work, and the guys at the gym as he finished cooking the paella.

"Do you like to cook?" he asked.

I snorted. "Uh, no. Not really. Never was good at it, and they have these things called cafés and delis, restaurants and takeout. They do it all for me."

Kira grinned and shook his head. "Oh, right," he said. "Cop's diet of coffee and doughnuts, right? I forgot."

I rolled my eyes. "Coffee yes, doughnuts not so much."

He scrunched his nose. "Yeah, they're disgusting."

"Do you eat anything that's not good for you?" I asked. "You know, being a personal trainer and all and considering how fit you are, I presume you don't eat anything with trans fats."

"I do eat healthy," he defended himself. "But I'm still human. I will *always* eat pizza."

"Pizza is good."

Kira smiled warmly. "So, you and the other guys hang out much?"

"Yeah, they're like my brothers," I answered. "But they

have girlfriends... well, Tony's married, but they're all coupled up."

"And you... ?"

"I'm the playboy of the police department, remember?" I said, sipping my beer. "Different girl every weekend."

Kira's eyebrows flickered. "Those are lucky girls."

"Those are nonexistent girls." Then I admitted, "Well, I took a 'date' to a department formal dinner once. It was the sister of some official. She wanted the fame of being in the papers, and I needed something female to match my tie," I said, pretending to straighten an equally nonexistent tie. "I'm sorry, that wasn't funny."

Kira chuckled, but it faded pretty fast. "It must be kinda awful to go through that."

"Part of the deal, I guess." Then I asked, "You?"

"Well, my parents know I'm gay, but I'm not out at work, obviously. I've never had to publicly accessorize with something female, if that's what you're asking."

"Never?"

"Nope," he said with that sexy smile. "Knew I was into the male accessories from an early age."

I took a swig of my beer. "How early?"

"Since *Baywatch*."

I snorted. "*Baywatch*? Was Pamela Anderson just not doing it for you?"

Kira got a dreamy look in his eyes and sighed. "The Hoff..."

I burst out laughing. "Oh, my God! You're not ever supposed to admit that!"

Kira threw his head back and laughed. "Okay, so it wasn't the Hoff. It was the guy who played Cody. What can I say?" He stared at me and waggled his eyebrows. "I have a thing for blond hair and blue eyes."

I blushed at his words, and his eyes brightened as though he found me amusing. Thankfully he didn't leave me hanging too long. "Hey, can you pass me those plates?" he asked, pointing to the counter.

"Sure."

By the time we were sitting at the table, I was much more at ease around him. Despite being a little embarrassed, he made me feel comfortable. Distracted, but comfortable.

I still got lost when I looked at him. He took a mouthful of rice, and I was transfixed by the fork between his lips. He smiled as he chewed and swallowed. "Are you gonna eat it or just watch me eat mine?" he asked, clearly amused.

Embarrassed, I shook my head and quickly shoved a forkful into my mouth. And oh my God, it was so fucking good. I groaned. He grinned. "This is really good," I told him with a mouthful of food.

"You sound surprised," he laughed.

I swallowed and amended quickly, "Oh, no. I just meant this is better than a restaurant could do."

He smirked as he ate. "Family recipe."

"Spanish?" I'd wondered about his heritage, whether he was more Asian or European.

He nodded. "My dad's Spanish, my mom's Japanese. I figured I'd play it safe with paella instead of sashimi."

I *thought* he was joking. It was kind of hard to tell, he smiled all the time. I shrugged at him. "I like sashimi too," I told him as I scooped up another forkful of rice. "But this is divine."

He grinned proudly. "I'm glad you like it."

We stared at each other then, and neither one of us spoke. I just looked at him. His dark, perfect eyes, his perfect lips...

His perfect, split, swollen lip.

"I'm sorry about your lip."

His hand automatically touched his mouth. "I'm not."

I raised my eyebrows in question, and he laughed. "I got you to agree to dinner with me."

I chuckled and gave him a nod. "That you did."

He picked up his beer bottle and clinked it to mine. "To split lips and dinner dates."

I couldn't help but smile as I tapped my bottle to his.

Then Kira started talking about how he'd got into fitness, how he'd traveled, and how he'd gotten started working at the gym. "I did sports at school and was always active or doing something. So it was a natural progression for me to get into fitness. My parents got me into karate when I was a kid. I was always getting into fights."

"What for?"

"The shape of my eyes, the color of my skin, the fact that I was gay," he said, matter-of-factly. "They didn't need any reasons." He took a mouthful of food and swallowed before he spoke again. "So in about my second year of high school, my parents took me to karate. It was good for a few years, but I progressed toward kickboxing, and... well, let's just say, I only got picked on once after that."

"What happened?"

"The guy who'd been picking on me for years lined me up in the locker room after gym. It'd been a while since he'd had a go at me, and I'd just assumed he'd found someone else to bully. He said I must have been working out to impress one of the guys. He shoved me a bit, and I warned him not to. But he didn't listen."

I smiled. "What did you do to him?"

Kira put his hands up in a mock arrest. "Nothing, officer, I swear. I don't know how he got to be lying on the floor with a broken nose and all unconscious like that. He must have tripped or something."

I laughed. "You got him?"

"He got what he deserved," Kira said with a shrug. "I'm not one to advocate violence, really. But he stopped picking on other kids after that too."

"Did you get into trouble?"

He shook his head. "The gym coach that came in knew I'd been bullied by that jerk for two years, so he kinda let it go. He told me later he'd wished he'd seen me do it. Not to catch me out or anything, but to watch that guy get his ass handed to him."

Then he told me about the kickboxing training he did and how he'd ended up applying for the job at Chris' gym for the supervisor's position.

I found myself enthralled by his story, his voice, and the way his neck muscles moved under the collar of his shirt. Then I noticed, a little late, that he'd stopped talking.

I'd been caught staring again.

He lifted his eyebrows and chuckled.

Embarrassed, I huffed out a breath, and I could feel heat creep over my cheeks. Jesus. I shook my head and looked down to the table. Figuring I could use the distraction, I started to clean up.

"Leave it," he said.

"You cooked, I clean," I told him. "Fair's fair."

I put the dirty plates in the sink and turned the water on as I looked through the cupboard under the sink for the detergent. When I found it, I looked up, and he was watching me. I busied myself by filling the sink and starting to wash up, and without a word, Kira picked up a dishtowel and started to dry.

He was right beside me. I could feel the heat of his

body. I could smell his cologne, his deodorant, his scent. I tried to concentrate on what I was doing, but by the time I was done and wiped down the sink, I knew this was it.

I knew if he touched me or kissed me, I'd have crossed the work/personal-life boundary with him. I'd be risking my comfortable, albeit closeted life.

I could have quite easily thanked him for dinner and made an excuse to leave. But I didn't want to.

When I looked at him, he gave me a shy smile... God, those fucking lips.

I turned back to the sink, trying to get myself together. His voice startled me. "If you want to leave, just say so."

I turned and looked at him. My heart was hammering, my mouth was dry, and I had to swallow so I could speak. "I don't want to leave."

He stepped closer to me and reached his hand up to the side of my face. "I don't want you to go," he said quietly. And oh-so-fucking slowly, he leaned in and pressed his lips to mine.

I couldn't move. I couldn't breathe.

His lips moved against mine, just a fraction, and then he pulled away. There was hurt and confusion in his eyes. He thought I didn't want this. "Don't you... ?"

"Too much," I said without thinking. "I want this too much."

Then my hands were on his face, around his neck, and I kissed him. Oh God, how I kissed him.

My lips opened his, and my tongue invaded his mouth. His lips, his tongue, his taste.

He groaned. That sound... my God, that sound.

Then his hands were on me and his arms were around me. I could feel him, all of him. It felt so fucking good. Desire. His need, hard against mine.

Just when I thought I didn't want this to ever end, he pulled his mouth from mine.

I was so torn. I wanted him to take me to bed. I wanted that with him. But I wanted something more. I wanted to get to know him, I wanted *that* with him. I knew it was far too soon to be thinking relationship, but I wanted something more with him. Once wouldn't ever be enough.

Like he understood, he smiled. "Whew," he exhaled with a laugh. "That... um... I thought for a minute I'd read the wrong signs. I thought at first when you didn't kiss me back..."

I chuckled, a little embarrassed at my reaction to him. "It's not very often I'm rendered catatonic by a kiss."

He laughed. "You certainly weren't catatonic the second time."

I blushed again. Jesus, what was it about this guy?

He touched the side of my face with the pad of his thumb. "So the city's toughest cop isn't that tough after all," he murmured. "In fact, he's quite shy." He leaned in and pressed his lips to my already heated cheek. "This blush gives you away."

I didn't answer. Well, I couldn't answer, the words wouldn't come.

"Normally, I'd um...," he started with a shrug. "Well, normally I'd just ask you if you wanted to fuck." My eyes widened at his blatant words, and he smiled. "But I don't want to."

Oh. I felt the stab of disappointment twist in my gut.

"Oh, no," he said, alarmed. He wrapped his hand around my jaw and pulled my face toward his. "What I meant is that yes, I want that. I *really* want that." He pecked my lips with his. "But I want to get to know you too."

Oh. I huffed out a breath, relieved. I nodded. "Me too."

He grinned and kissed me soundly. Sweetly. When he pulled away, he took a step back, putting some distance between us. He chuckled and shook his head—he seemed as surprised by the attraction between us as I was.

"I have classes in the morning," he said. "But I'm free for lunch."

He wanted to see me tomorrow. I smiled, but then I remembered..." I, uh, I can't risk being seen out with a guy. I'm sorry."

"That's okay," he said genuinely. "You can bring lunch here. I'll be home by noon."

I couldn't help but smile. "Deal."

"Look, Matt," he whispered. "I know you're worried about the guys finding out. But I promise you this." He looked at me so intently. "They won't hear it from me."

I didn't know what it was about him, but his eyes—I could see only honesty in them. I nodded, and before I was plagued by thoughts of *it won't be long before he's sick of hiding,* he held out his hand. "Can I have your phone?" He laughed at my expression and rolled his eyes. "Are all cops so suspicious?"

Well, yes. Mostly. But I handed him my cell phone regardless. He worked his thumb over the screen and showed me. He'd put in his number under the name Kira. "Now I know you've got my number," he said. He pressed the call button, and the phone on the counter, his cell phone, rang. He grinned. "And now I've got yours. If anyone reads the name Kira," he went on to say, "they'll just think it's one more female admirer."

"Thank you, Kira," I said, and he smiled when I called him by his given name. Though I wasn't exactly sure what I was thanking him for—dinner, for taking a chance on me, for being so understanding. Or all three. "You're being very... gracious."

He shook his head. "Like I said before, we're keeping the same secret."

I stared at him. I could see the rise and fall of his chest, but I was lost in his eyes. I touched the side of his face, and his lips curled upwards.

The words were out before I could stop them. "You have such a beautiful smile." I kissed his smiling lips, just a quick peck, and then another. "I should go," I told him. "If I don't go now, you'll be cooking me breakfast."

He chuckled, and his hand rested on my hip. "I wouldn't mind at all."

He smiled when I groaned. "Don't tempt me."

He laughed quietly, but his smile died and his eyes intensified. He murmured, "What is it about you?"

Then it was my turn to chuckle. "I was just thinking the same thing."

And somehow, with the self-control and willpower I hadn't known I had, I kissed him once more and left.

CHAPTER FIVE

I WAS STANDING in front of his door at five past twelve. I'd collected an array of food from the deli, and not knowing what he liked and what he didn't, I'd just grabbed a bit of everything.

I'd also done nothing but think about this guy since I'd left him last night. I'd jerked off twice that morning already, and the thought of seeing him again made my dick twitch.

I knocked again, and there was no answer. Shit.

I checked my phone. There were no messages from him. I briefly considered calling him but thought that might make me look desperate. Maybe a text would suffice? Just when I was considering texting him, he came running around the corner.

"Oh, hey!" he said with a surprised smile.

Fuck me.

He was still wearing his gym gear, still sweaty and looking a little flushed. God, my cock throbbed. I gaped at him before I could think to speak. "Hey."

"Chris wanted me to do an extra class," he explained. "Sorry I'm late."

I looked him over, blatantly appreciating his body. "I don't mind."

He grinned at me as he opened the door to his apartment. "I normally shower at work, but I didn't want you to think I'd stood you up," he said, holding the door open for me to walk inside. "I'll just grab a quick shower now, if you want to set up lunch." He looked to the deli bags in my hands. "Help yourself to anything you need in the kitchen."

He left me standing alone and a little out of place in his living room. I walked into the kitchen, and then he was suddenly behind me. I turned to face him, and he quickly pecked my lips with his. "I forgot to say hello," he said with a smile. "I won't be long."

He left me alone for the second time, but this time I smiled. I found some plates and heard the water start in the bathroom. I tried really, *really* hard not to think of him being wet and naked just a few yards from me. How the water would run down his body, how his muscles, his skin would look wet...

Shaking my head to clear it, I concentrated on what I was doing instead. And by the time I had lunch all spread out on the table with plates and cutlery, I thought I had my body's reaction to him under control.

That was until he walked out.

Fuck.

A freshly showered Kira was just as hot as a sweaty, flushed Kira. He was wearing a simple, plain white polo and khakis. Nothing extraordinary but very remarkable, indeed.

"Jeez," he said, looking at the table. "How many people did you buy lunch for?"

But I was stuck staring at him. Fuck me, he was beautiful.

He looked at me expectantly. "Um," I started, trying to remember his question. "I wasn't sure what you liked, so I bought a little of everything."

He grinned at me. "You okay? You look a little flustered."

I blushed, giving myself away, and chuckled at my own embarrassment.

Kira picked up an olive and popped it into his mouth. He smiled as he chewed. "Mmm, these are good. I'm starving."

He sat himself at the dining table and started talking about the deli food, his local grocer, and favorite recipes. And just like that, he put me at ease. But his eyes danced as he talked and a smile played at his lips, as though he knew how I struggled to be coherent around him. I thought I amused him.

I tried not to notice how his smile lit his whole face, or the way his shirt teased his collar bones, or how the white of his shirt contrasted beautifully with the color of his skin. I tried really hard not to notice how well defined his arms were, how strong his hands were.

Despite my slow start at conversation, we talked about anything and everything. It was so easy, and I had no doubt this could go somewhere. I could see myself spending a lot of time with him.

"My mom and dad are a lot of fun," he said. "There's never a dull moment. They've always been pretty cool with everything. What about you?"

"It was only ever me and my mom," I told him. "She passed away when I was seventeen."

"Oh, shit. I'm sorry."

"It's okay," I reassured him. "It's been ten years."

"You've been on your own since then?"

"Well, kind of. I've had my police family."

"I can't imagine," he said quietly. "I can't imagine not having my family." Then he took another mouthful of his salad. "Any brothers or sisters?"

"No. You?"

"No, Mom couldn't have any more kids after me, so I'm it. The one and only."

I bit into some fresh Turkish bread. "No pressure, then?"

Kira smiled and shook his head. "Nah, not from my folks. They're fairly laid back with everything." He speared some sliced pastrami and bit his lip. "Can I ask you something?"

I was suddenly nervous. "Sure."

"What did you do when your mom died?" he asked. "I mean, you were only seventeen."

I took a deep breath and told him what only a handful of other people knew. "I had two cops come tell me my mom was in a car wreck. They asked me who they could call, and well, there wasn't anyone. I was only three weeks from turning eighteen, and I inherited the house." I explained the house was kinda big, but after my mom died, it had never really felt like home. "I just live there," I told him with a shrug. "But it's not really a home."

Then very unlike me, I kept talking. "I was still in school and had an afternoon job and told them I wasn't leaving the house, so they finally caved in and said I could stay, and they came to check on me every day. They really helped me and supported me." I sipped my drink and shrugged. "I joined the police the day I turned eighteen. They've been my family since."

He listened like I held the secrets to the world. I felt a

bit foolish for spilling my life history to a man I hardly knew, but there was just something about him.

"Do you get lonely?" he asked. "Being on your own so much?" Personal questions obviously didn't faze him.

I shook my head. "Not really. I mean, I rarely have any time off, and if the boss ever makes us take a few days' break, we end up at someone's place playing cards and cooking out or I use that time to catch up on sleep."

Kira smiled as he ate. "So not much time for boyfriends?"

I blushed again. Fuck. "Not really. Like I said before, my job isn't exactly relationship-friendly."

"But you're working on it?"

I smiled at him. "Maybe."

"Just maybe?" he asked with a smirk. "I thought it was doing better than just a maybe."

I couldn't stop the grin. "Well, it could be. Not sure yet. It will depend solely on what sports teams he follows."

Kira grinned back at me. "Which sport?"

"Football, basketball, baseball, hockey."

He answered immediately. "Steelers, Lakers, Dodgers and the Kings."

I couldn't help but smile at him. "Well, the Steelers I'll accept, the Lakers yes, the Dodgers maybe, but the Kings could be an unfortunate deal-breaker."

He laughed, but then he pointed to the food on the table. "Just as well you bought lunch."

"Yeah, well, I wasn't exactly sure what to bring. I've never exactly had a great deal of second dates either," I admitted. "I mean, there were plenty of second *encounters*, but not *dates*."

Kira waggled his eyebrows and grinned. "So, what

you're saying is, I must be something special if you're breaking your own rules for me."

I willed myself not to blush, not to give me away. I hid my embarrassment with a laugh and pretended my plate was the most interesting thing in the world.

Kira just smiled. Eventually, he started to pack up what was left of lunch, and as he carried it into the kitchen, I followed him. But after all the talking we'd done, when he turned in the kitchen to find me just inches away, all conversation stopped. We were so close I wondered if he could hear my heart thumping in my chest. When he smiled, I was sure he could.

He licked his lips, his perfect lips, and I stared at them. I could hardly see the mark where I hit him yesterday. "Your lip's better," I said.

He smiled and said, "No one punched me in the mouth today."

But he was staring at me with those so-brown eyes, and when he licked his lips again, I knew he was about to kiss me.

"If you kiss me," I said quietly, "I won't be going home any time soon."

"Good," he murmured before he held my face and pressed his mouth to mine. Sweet Jesus, how he kissed me.

His hands, his lips, his tongue.

When I slid my arms around him and pulled us together, I could feel his desire, his want, his need hard against my hip. He groaned and kissed me harder. I melted into him, his body, his warmth, his strength.

That kiss was all I'd thought about. *He* was all I'd thought about.

I wanted him. I wanted him to have me.

Sliding my hands over the muscles of his back, I slid my

fingers into his hair, and I pulled his mouth from mine. "Bedroom" was all I could say.

He rested his forehead against mine. His chest was heaving; his lips were swollen. "Matt," he said, barely a breath. "If I take you into my room, I will taste you." My breath hitched, and my belly tightened. He cradled my face and brushed his lips against mine. "I will have you."

"Please." God, it sounded like I was begging. Maybe I was. "Oh, God. Please."

He grabbed my hand, led me out of the kitchen, and took me to his bedroom. And my nervousness around him disappeared. I was so sure about this.

This time when he kissed me, it was different. Slower, harder, deeper. He took his time undressing me, as though he was savoring every inch of skin he uncovered, kissing and licking as he explored. When I was lying down on his bed, completely at his mercy, his lips were trailing from my chest down, down, until I was gripping the sheets at my side.

I couldn't not watch him. It was the most erotic thing I'd ever seen. When his perfect lips opened to take my cock into his mouth, I was lost to the sensation. His warm, wet mouth was all encompassing and sucking as his tongue was swirling and lapping, and his fingers were slick and delicious, pressing and probing.

I was groaning shamelessly, writhing under his touch. His fingers were inside me. One, two, moving and pumping as his mouth worked up and down my cock. Sucking and sliding, his mouth was setting my blood on fire; I was warmed right through.

Then he sucked hard and pumped me, once, twice. And I was lost. I couldn't think. I couldn't speak. I fisted his hair, trying to warn him, but it only made him look up at me. His dark eyes and his perfect lips around my cock did me in.

Then he moaned.

I came so fucking hard.

The world disappeared, all sight, all sound. The only thing there was... was his mouth... and tongue, and his moans as he drank what I gave him.

Then he was gone. I tried to open my eyes and lift my hand, but it was too heavy. I heard him chuckle, heard the tear of foil, and then, like I weighed nothing, he flipped my boneless body over.

I was face down on his bed. He was between my thighs, his hands were at my sides, and he leaned over my back. I could feel his cock pressing against my ass, so I lifted my hips for him and he pressed into me.

Oh, fuck.

He pushed and pushed until he was all the way inside me. Only then did he seem to breathe. Falling forward, so he was lying on top of me, he ground his hips into my ass— his long, hot cock was so far inside me.

Panting, he ran his hands up my sides, hooking his fingers under my shoulders, and then he started to thrust into me. It was everything I'd imagined it would be.

"So good," he mumbled into the back of my neck. "Oh, fuck. Matt...," he moaned into my shoulder as he pushed harder, faster. Then he kissed behind my ear and down the back of my neck, and he was thrusting so hard, so good. I lifted my ass to meet him, granting him better access, deeper, longer. Then he groaned long and loud, "Oh, gonna come." And I could feel his cock swell and empty into the condom inside me.

He slumped down on top of me, resting his entire weight on my back. In between ragged breaths, he kissed my shoulder, my neck, and the back of my head before he pulled out of me. He rolled us onto our sides, wrapped his arms completely around me, and we drifted off to sleep.

I hadn't been kidding when I'd told him in his kitchen if he kissed me I wouldn't be leaving any time soon. Because it wasn't until almost midnight on Sunday night I dragged myself out of his bedroom, after an entire weekend of sex, and made myself go home.

CHAPTER SIX

OVER THE NEXT FOUR WEEKS, we saw each other almost constantly. When I wasn't working, I stayed at his place. He'd been to my house a few times, but considering it was likely any of the guys I worked with could just turn up uninvited, we opted to stay at his place. We'd spend daylight hours talking and laughing and nighttime hours exploring each other's bodies. We kept our boxing sessions as per normal. The guys from work liked him and treated him like one of the boys.

No one suspected a thing.

Except for Mitch. He knew something was different. I was happier, he said. He'd catch me smiling, and he'd call me on it. He presumed, like they all did, it was a woman behind my newfound happiness, but I admitted to nothing.

I didn't deny or confirm Mitch's suspicions, which according to him confirmed his suspicions.

He'd been my partner for two years, so of course he'd notice. But he also knew I was a private guy, so thankfully he didn't push me on it. I most certainly didn't bring it up.

But he commented on how "she" must be someone special because he'd never seen me so happy.

And apart from the "she" distinction, he was very fucking right. I'd never been so happy.

It was a very lazy Sunday morning in bed—we'd been together for four weeks—and I told Kira how Mitch could see how happy I was. I explained how he kept making "she" comments about the presumed female reason behind my smile.

I told him, "He says he knows I'm seeing someone because of how much easier I am to get along with."

Kira smiled, and as he traced his fingers along my jaw, he said, "You mean, you're less sexually frustrated."

I laughed and nodded. "That too."

He hooked his leg over mine. "It has nothing to do with how your dreamy boyfriend cooks you dinner or puts up with your crap taste in movies."

Dreamy boyfriend.

Boyfriend.

We'd not used labels before. "Boyfriend, huh?"

For the first time, I saw doubt in his eyes. Normally so confident and forthright, he swallowed and nodded. With hesitation and hope in his eyes, he said, "Well, I, um... kinda thought..."

I smiled as I pulled his arm so he slid on top of me, and I hooked my legs around his thighs. "Well, boyfriend," I said with a smile in my voice, "why don't you fuck me like a boyfriend should?"

He chuckled into my neck, playfully biting me, nipping and kissing all the skin he could reach. When he finally, *finally* pushed into me, his hands gripped me as he buried himself, so deep, so right. His fingers dug into my skin as he held me too tightly, but still not tight enough. His lips and his tongue were fucking my mouth while he fucked my ass with his dick, and he consumed all of me.

He pushed my legs higher, almost folding me in half, and every inch of him was buried in me. He rocked and ground his hips, drilling me deeper and deeper, and I held his face between my hands. I whispered against his lips, "You feel so good inside me."

He grunted and shuddered, his whole body convulsing as he stilled over me, filling the condom again and again.

Then he led me into the bathroom and into the shower. "One orgasm between us isn't anywhere near enough," Kira declared. He dropped to his knees in front of me, and I held onto the walls at my sides. And as the warm water washed over my head, he cupped my balls in one hand and pumped my shaft in the other while he sucked on the head.

Except I took my hands off the walls to grip his hair as my cock erupted in his throat, and we overbalanced or fell or slid or something because we ended up on the floor in the shower, a jumbled mess of limbs and laughter.

We were still chuckling as we made it to the kitchen to find something to eat when there was a knock at the door.

I froze.

Just like that, this perfect little bubble I'd lived in for the last four weeks burst. I couldn't be seen here. There was no explanation I could give to justify why I was at Kira's place.

"Expecting someone?"

Kira looked at me, and he could tell I was worried.

Then a female voice said, "Kira! You home?"

Kira groaned. "It's just my mom."

Oh. His mom.

Did boyfriends meet moms? I guessed they did. Well, I guessed I was about to.

Kira disappeared, and by the time I got to the kitchen

door, in barreled a tiny, Japanese woman. She had straight, jet-black hair to her shoulders, and she was letting Kira have a piece of her mind. She pointed her finger up at him. "You not call us or come to see us in weeks!" Then she threw up her hands and spoke in broken English. "What for? Why you not call me? I worry sick, Kira."

Kira looked at me, trying not to smile. "Ah, Mom, I'd like you to meet Matthew Elliott," he said. Then he grinned. "My boyfriend. Matt, this is my mother, Yumi."

Yumi turned to look at me. Her eyes were wide and her mouth open. "Oh," she said quietly. "Oh, you the boy off the television."

I crossed the room and extended my hand to her. "Nice to meet you."

She took my hand in a small, but firm grip. "So, you the reason why my Kira disappear for four weeks?"

"Um..."

Kira interrupted, saving me. "Mom, where's Dad?"

"He park the car. I came up to see if you are still alive." She threw her hands up in the air. "Could have been dead for all I know."

Kira grinned and rolled his eyes. "It's okay, Mom. I've been in very safe hands." Then he leaned in and whispered to her, "Matt's a policeman."

Oh my God. I couldn't believe he'd just said that!

Yumi swatted her son's arm. "Don't want details." Kira laughed, and Yumi shook her head at him. "Why you not call me to tell me you got a boyfriend?"

He didn't answer her question, but pacified her with a hug instead. She grumbled at him, but she smiled just as there was another knock at the door. Kira went to the front door and came back with a man who could only be his father; I knew where Kira got his height. The man who walked in was tall, about six foot three, dark hair, olive skin.

"Matt, this is my dad, Salvidore Franco. We call him Sal," Kira explained, but then quickly moved his hands, and I realized a little belatedly, he was signing. Kira's father was deaf.

I shook his hand, mumbled my hellos, completely unprepared to be meeting the parents. I didn't think I'd ever "met the parents" before. It was a little daunting.

Kira's father, Sal, quickly signed something to which Yumi laughed, and Kira grinned at me. "My dad says you look taller on TV."

I snorted and could feel my face heat with embarrassment as the three of them looked at me and smiled.

Over the next two hours, I came to realize Kira's family was very close, very open about everything and very, very funny. I knew now why Kira was always smiling, because his mom and dad were too.

Yumi, all of her five feet, still nagged Kira about being so distracted and for at least not calling to let them know he was okay. Then she turned on me, making me promise to make him call.

I quickly deduced Sal read lips, because they didn't sign everything they said, but when Sal had something to say, Kira translated the sign language for me. Sal told me when Kira didn't at least phone his mother, he was the one who suffered. Sal grinned, Kira laughed, and Yumi scowled at them both.

Yumi talked almost non-stop, making up for the fact that Sal didn't say a word. I liked them. They were very familial, and it was obvious they adored their son. We were invited for lunch the next weekend, and when I explained my job wasn't exactly Monday to Friday, Yumi simply clicked her tongue. "Then you come for dinner through the week."

She was a tenacious little thing, and while it was obvious Kira got his height and looks from his dad, he got the "take no crap" kickboxing attitude from his mother.

Early afternoon soon became late afternoon, and just as Yumi suggested dinner, my phone beeped.

"It's work. I gotta go in," I told them, reading the message.

"More bad guys?" Kira asked.

I nodded. "There's always more bad guys."

I wasn't really ready for this weekend to be over, but I had to bid them farewell regardless. I shook Sal's hand and told Yumi I promised to keep Kira in line.

Kira laughed and kissed me right on the lips, right in front of them. Before I had time to be embarrassed, Yumi grinned up at her son. "I like him."

Kira looked at me and smiled. "I'm rather fond of him too."

I stammered my goodbyes, feeling every bit the idiot, and grinned all the way to my place to get changed. Then I grinned all the way to work. Not that I'd told Kira how I felt, but if by "fond of" he meant "can't stop thinking about," or "wanted to spend all my time with," or "completely besotted with," then yes, I was rather *fond* of him too.

CHAPTER SEVEN

I WALKED into the office to find Mitch, Kurt, and Tony already there. I still couldn't help but grin at work, and of course they noticed. Kurt nodded smugly at me. "You're awfully happy to be called into work on a Sunday night."

"You're last here," Tony added. "You're never the last one here."

I ignored them, and Mitch smiled at me, but he said nothing. He knew there was a reason behind my smile, and for him that was enough. I guessed he was just happy I was happy. I smiled back at him, leaning against the table next to him, waiting for Ross.

Our boss, Commanding Officer Ross Berkman, walked in. He was a tall, well-built man with a gray military-style haircut and a no-nonsense stare that scared the shit out of the probationaries. He was a hard-ass, strict, but fair. I liked him.

"Someone's taken over Tomic's cartel," he said, no introduction, no pleasantries. "The word on the street is as though Tomic never left. Just business as usual. Someone's just picked up right where the slimebag left off."

I could feel that stab of instinct in my gut. It burned and twisted and sent gooseflesh up my arms. I'd *known* something wasn't right with that case.

Mitch looked at me as though he could read my mind, but before either one of us could say anything, Ross gave Tony and Kurt their orders. "Milic, Webber, see what you can find out in the red light district." Then Ross looked at me and Mitch. "Elliott, Seaton, see what your snitch has to say. I don't need to remind you"—Ross reminded us anyway —"Tomic's court case is in just over two months. We need this case watertight or the bastard will walk." The older man looked at the four of us and said, "Be careful," and walked out the door.

So we did what we always did. Kurt and Tony went in one direction, Mitch and me in the other, and when we were done, we'd meet up at HQ and trade information.

On our way to the wharves, Mitch kept looking at me and smiling.

"What?" I asked him.

"So," he said with a grin. "Gonna give me a name?"

"Ferret."

He snorted. "Not the snitch's name, smartass. The reason behind that smile."

My chest tightened, and my stomach knotted. I rolled my eyes at him and decided looking out the window to the darkened streets was safer than answering.

"Oh, come on," he said with a frustrated sigh. "Jesus, Matt. I'm your fucking partner. The least you can do is give me a name."

So this was it. A sliver of information. I risked giving myself away if I did tell him, but I risked more by not giving him this. It was just a name. A name that most people associated with a woman, not a man. Surely this wouldn't out me...

I looked at Mitch and swallowed hard. I tried to speak, but I needed to push the air out to make the sound, and still nothing would come.

I looked back out the window. It was easier if I didn't look at him.

My voice was quiet, but he heard me just fine. "Kira."

"Keira?" he repeated. "As in Keira Knightley?" Then his eyes went huge, and he cried, "Oh fuck, it's not *actually* Keira Knightley, is it? Is *that* the reason for the secrecy?"

I chuckled, instantly relieved. "No, it's not Keira Knightley."

He laughed and nodded. Then he smiled at me. "That wasn't so hard, was it?"

I finally breathed, but my heart was still hammering. He had no idea just how hard that had been. I smiled again, kinda glad to have gotten it out. Then he asked, "Does Keira have a last name?"

"Oh no," I said, shaking my head. "You're not running background checks, plate checks, credit checks, license checks—"

Mitch laughed. "I wouldn't do that."

I stared at him. He so fucking would.

He rolled his eyes petulantly. "Well, okay... maybe I would have." Then he was quiet for a minute as he concentrated on driving. "So," he started again with a smirk, "does your Keira look anything like Keira Knightley?"

I answered by rolling my eyes at him.

We pulled up along the poorly lit section of industrial wharves, and I could count five human shadows scattered along the walls. I knew Mitch would have done the same, sizing up possible threats. As we got out of the car, we walked toward the lone streetlight, where two hookers were waiting.

They knew we were cops. We didn't try and hide it. But we weren't here for them, and they knew that too. It wasn't the first time we'd been down there.

"Hello, ladies," I said pleasantly. "Seen Ferret around?"

"What's it to you?" the first hooker asked. Even the dim streetlight didn't hide her tired face, her pallid skin marked by drugs, rough nights, and time.

These women talked two languages: sex and drugs. So Mitch answered her, amused. "You know, Ferret's been 'doing us favors'"—he blatantly grabbed his crotch—"when the need arises."

I tried not to smile.

The second hooker spoke up. "You don't need Ferret for that, sugar. I could help you out right now. Blowjobs are my specialty. Ten bucks for one of ya, fifteen for both."

I repressed a shudder. Mitch wasn't so amused now. "Ferret? Where is he?"

The first hooker held out her hand, waiting. I handed her a ten-dollar bill for the information, and she replied with a nod toward the end wharf. "He passed through before, 'bout an hour ago, I s'pose. Went that way."

"Wearin' a long, brown coat," the second woman said. "'Bout two sizes too big for him. Musta borrowed it from some Joe."

I snorted at the likelihood of that. Yeah, borrowed. Like he'd ever give something back.

I handed the second woman another ten for her troubles, and Mitch and I both headed toward the direction of the end wharf.

The old warehouses on these docks provided shelter for the homeless but were cesspools for drugs, hooking, and death wishes. The drug runners and dealers had caught wind of us the second we pulled up and had disappeared, for now anyway. We passed a few other people, either too high to realize we were cops or long past the point of caring.

But we eventually found our man outside, along the far wall that faced the water, finalizing some deal with a guy who scurried off when we arrived.

Ferret was a small, scrawny guy with pointy, pinched features whose nickname of Ferret described him perfectly. Just as the second hooker had said, he was sporting a new brown coat, which made him look even more rodent-like.

Ferret was maybe in his early twenties and had been hooking since he was about sixteen. He was smart enough to have survived this long. He saw what went on, heard street-talk that rumbled underground, knew when to lie low, and knew when to run. He'd been our snitch, our eyes and ears on the streets, for over a year.

"Gentlemen," he greeted us, nervously. "In your car tonight? Or shall I blow you both here?" he asked, loud enough for the listening ears to hear.

No doubt, someone was always listening.

Without answering, we turned, and he followed. When we got back to the car, we sat on either side of him in the backseat. The windows were tinted enough, and we were far enough from the streetlight, prying eyes couldn't see what we were doing. To them, we might very well just be clients. In the darkened car, he might very well have been sucking our dicks.

He was all twitchy, adding to his ferret-like features, and I wondered how much was drug-induced and how much was just him. He reeked. The smell was rank.

"Wassup?" he asked.

"Tomic," I answered, short and simple. "What's the word on the street?"

"You tell me!" the little man said. "He got hauled in with all that ice, then twenty-four hours later, he's back out again!"

"What?" Mitch asked, as confused as me.

"All that money must have paid for some good lawyer," he said, still twitching, and his knees were bouncing.

"Tomic isn't out," I explained. "He's still behind bars at County."

Ferret blinked twice, then twitched again. "I saw him," he said. Then he closed his eyes tight and shook his head. "I saw him."

I repressed a sigh. I wanted to ask him how many drugs he'd had today, or when the last time was he ate, or slept... or showered. Instead, I asked him, "Where did you see him?"

He scrubbed at his face. "Um..."

Mitch saw exactly what I saw. "Ferret, what day is it today?"

Ferret looked up at him sharply. "I dunno, man!" he cried. "How the fuck would I know? Don't exactly get the *LA Times* delivered round these parts."

"Ferret." I said his name slowly. "I can't pay you if you don't tell us anything—"

He cut me off. "Next block over," he said out of the blue. "Up on Fourth. That's where I saw him."

Mitch sighed, and even in the darkened car, I could see him roll his eyes, fed up. Now he was just telling us anything so we'd give him money. Ferret looked at me—his eyes were wide, glassy and empty. He licked his dry lips. "Tomic's men are still workin'," he said with a shrug. "But I stay away from 'em. They come in, and I'm gone."

"Was there someone working *with* Tomic?" I asked,

though I wasn't sure why. He was hardly making any sense, and I'd asked him this before.

He looked at me and blinked. His whole face twitched. "I told ya, not that I ever saw. No word of anyone else. His men answered to Tomic. Everyone answered to Tomic. No one else."

"His men are still working?" I asked him, clarifying something he'd said before.

Ferret nodded hard. "Mean sons of bitches. I hide real good when they come round."

He started looking out the window, scouting his surroundings, and I knew our time was up. It'd be too suspicious if he were away too long.

I slipped a fifty out of my pocket and handed it to him. "Get something to eat," I told him, knowing damn well he wouldn't. Without another word, Mitch and I opened the doors and got out. Ferret scampered out after me, looked back at us, wiped his mouth for effect as though he just gave two blowjobs, and he was gone.

We headed back to HQ, not really any better off. Kurt and Tony arrived not too long after us.

"Think he's losing it," Mitch told the others when we told them what Ferret had to say. "Drugs have got him."

I sighed. "He's never let us down yet," I countered quietly. "But maybe there is some truth somewhere in his madness."

Mitch leaned back in his chair and frowned. "Matt…"

I nodded. Ferret was losing it—he was as high as a kite tonight and not making a great deal of sense. "I know. I know."

"What's the word on your side?" Mitch asked Kurt and Tony.

Both men exhaled at the same time. "Just what the boss said," Tony explained. "Business as usual."

Kurt agreed. "We take down one ring, and another just pops up in its place." He rubbed his hands over his face. "There's always another asshole wanting to make a name for himself as the kingpin."

"But not Tomic," I said, frustrated.

Mitch shook his head at me. "It's not Tomic. The bastard's behind bars, Matt." He was clearly sick of having this conversation with me. "Ferret doesn't even know what day it is."

"Right," our boss said with a finality that meant we were done with this for tonight. "It's two a.m. Go home."

We watched Berkman walk into his office in silence. When his office door shut behind him, Mitch, Kurt, and Tony all stood up, but when I grabbed the file on my desk and opened it, obviously not going anywhere, Mitch sighed. "Let it go, Matt." He clapped his hand on my shoulder. "Go home. Go to Keira's."

Kurt and Tony stopped in their tracks and turned to look at me.

I stared at Mitch. "Nice, partner. Real nice. So much for partners' code of silence."

"Keira?" Kurt said with wide eyes and a bewildered smile. "As in Keira Knightley?"

Mitch laughed. "Nah, apparently it's not."

Tony looked at Mitch. "Does she have an English accent? Because then we'd know for sure."

Mitch was still grinning. "No, I never spoke to her." Then my partner looked at me. "Is she English?"

I cleared my throat and shook my head. "Um, Japanese..." I stopped myself short on adding Spanish. I didn't know why I'd even told them that much.

All three men stared at me. Mitch grinned, then looked at Kurt and Tony. "This is new. I didn't know that before now."

"Didn't know what?" Berkman asked, walking in on the conversation.

Kurt was quick to spill. "Matt's new love, Keira, is Japanese."

Berkman looked at me for a long second, then shrugged like he couldn't give a shit and kept walking.

Kurt and Tony both joked with Mitch, and I could hear him explaining as they walked toward the elevator how he'd only got a first name and now he had a nationality. "I'll know who it is soon enough, boys."

I rolled my eyes, even though they didn't see it, picked up the Tomic case file, and started at the beginning.

CHAPTER EIGHT

I CAUGHT a few hours sleep at my desk, enough to tide me over, and although I spoke to Kira on the phone, I didn't see him until Wednesday.

Finally getting my head out of paperwork, I kept my usual Wednesday gym appointment. When I walked into that boxing room, thank God no one else was in there because his smile was blinding.

I could tell he wanted to speak freely, or touch me, but considering where we were, he couldn't. "You look tired," he said quietly as he helped me strap my hands.

"I'm okay," I told him, tracing his fingers with mine. I spoke so quiet only he could hear. "I'm sorry I haven't been around."

"It's okay," he answered with a smile. But then he tapped my hands and quickly tapped my cheek. "I'll get good payback for sleeping alone."

I laughed. "So every time I have to work late, you're gonna kick my ass in here?"

He grinned. "Something like that." He stood in the middle of the floor, stretched his neck, shook out his arms and bounced on his toes. "Come on, Detective. Give it your best shot."

Just when I thought this was gonna hurt, he actually took it easy on me. We went through the usual one-two-jab sequences, but he habitually still lifted his right foot, his kickboxing foot.

I stepped back and dropped my hands. "Teach me kickboxing."

He lowered his hands, and he stood up straight. "Why?"

"I want to learn."

"You're too tired today."

I knew he was taking it easy on me because he knew I hadn't slept. "Do you think the guys I track down care if I'm tired?"

He didn't answer, but he still looked hesitant.

"Do you think drug dealers give a shit if I don't sleep?" I asked him. "In fact, it's when I'm most vulnerable that I should know how to defend myself properly."

He glared at me. I think he might have even growled, and I knew I'd won this one.

But fuck, he let me have it. He faced me in mirrored stances and showed me the basics. And little by little, he let fly, tapping my shin and thigh with his foot.

It fucking hurt.

He was glorious. He was so damn fast. And fit. Holy hell, he was fit. He barked instructions at me, and I had to admit, it was a bit of a turn-on.

I'd seen how commanding he could be in the bedroom. I'd seen how he took charge. It was fucking hot.

But the burning sting of his foot connecting with my calf and thigh ruined any chance of this being arousing.

When I knocked on his door at ten that night, he leaned against the frame and smiled at me. "How's the leg?"

I walked inside and toed off my shoes. "Sore, but thanks for asking."

He closed the door, leaned against it, and his smile twisted into a pout. "I'm sorry."

I walked up to him, right up to him, and pushed myself against him and kissed him, hard. He responded in kind, threading his hand around my neck while his tongue invaded my mouth, and I just melted into him. I just fucking melted.

I couldn't explain it. It was foreign to me. It was a feeling I couldn't describe, being with him. Sure, it was desire and heat, and want and need, push and pull.

But it was something else. Something I'd never really felt with anyone.

Safe. I felt safe with him. When I was with him, in his arms, kissing him, feeling his hands touch every inch of me, I felt as though I'd found home.

HE HAD me naked on his bed, after he'd made me come, and he was inspecting my leg and thigh where he'd kick-boxed me earlier. He gently rubbed the reddened skin, trailing soft kisses in his wake, and it amazed me how he could be so lethal, yet so gentle.

When he was certain my leg was okay, he made me come again. This time he was inside me, every inch of him, pushing magic buttons to spark fireworks behind my eyes. I came so hard I swore it jellified my bones.

When I could finally open my eyes, he had cleaned us up and had wrapped himself completely around me.

I kissed his bare shoulder and smiled into his skin. I wriggled into him just a little bit more, and his arms tightened around me. I breathed in the smell of him, the smell of us, and fell back into sleep with a smile.

———

I WOKE up to the bright California sun streaming through the window slats and a rather rude slap to my ass cheek.

I groaned and grumbled some obscenity at him, but Kira just laughed. "Up you get, sleepyhead. It's seven o'clock."

I groaned again, just for good measure, but threw back the cover and dragged myself to the bathroom.

When I made it to the kitchen in a pair of his boxers, he was sitting at the bench, eating his breakfast. He looked at what I was wearing, then back up to my face. "Help yourself to my clothes."

"I did."

He chuckled at me as I struggled to make myself coffee. "You should try a breakfast like mine."

I looked at what he was eating—granola, diced fruit, and yogurt—and my stomach turned. I groaned. "Mm-mm. Just coffee," my voice croaked.

He laughed at me again. He always found my morning grumpiness amusing. But every morning without fail, he started the coffee machine for me before I got up.

I took a sip and could feel it breathing life into me on a cellular level.

"You drink too much caffeine," he told me.

"You eat too healthy."

He laughed, smiling beautifully.

Then I remembered what I'd told Mitch the other night. I hadn't seen Kira since then. Oh, hell... "Hey, babe?"

He looked up at me, startled at the term of endearment. "Yes... *babe?*"

I couldn't help but smile, but I put my coffee down and looked at him. "Um, Mitch knows I'm seeing someone called Kira."

His smile died, and he put his spoon down. "Oh," he said, then cleared his throat, obviously uncomfortable with the whole idea. "And...?"

"He thinks I'm secretly dating Keira Knightley."

Kira snorted. "I should be offended! I'm so much prettier than she is."

I smiled at him, but then I told him seriously, "I had to tell him. They know I'm seeing someone, and he's been really good about me not giving details. But then when it was just us, he asked me for a name." I took Kira's hand and gave it a squeeze. "I wasn't going to tell him, but he asked. I can't lie to him. He's my partner. I mean, I go to his house for barbeques and stuff. I know all about his girlfriend, Anna. He tells me everything." Kira was looking at our joined hands, but he wasn't saying anything. "Babe, I swear, that's all he knows. Just the name."

Kira turned our hands over and gently squeezed my fingers. "Do you want to tell him about us?"

I blinked at his words, at what he was implying. "Come out, you mean?"

Kira nodded. "Like you said, he's your partner. You shouldn't have secrets."

"I've never lied to him," I said quietly, defiantly.

"Hey." Kira quickly stood up and stepped in front of me. He lifted my chin, so I looked at him. "I know that. I didn't mean you were lying to him. I just meant that if you want to tell him, then I'll support you."

I smiled, though it was weak at best. "I know what you meant," I replied softly. "Thank you. But I'm not sure. It can't be undone. Once I tell him, I can't take it back."

Kira nodded. "I know."

He did know. He knew *exactly* what I meant.

"But you know him," Kira said seriously, looking me right in the eyes. "You trust him."

"With my life."

Kira nodded once. "How do you honestly think he'll react?"

I shrugged hesitantly. "I'm not sure. He could be okay with it." I looked into Kira's dark, honest eyes. "But what if he's not? He's like a brother to me. I can't risk losing that."

Kira pecked my lips and then pulled me against him. He sighed deeply. "I can't decide for you. But if you want to tell him when the time is right, we'll deal with it then."

I smiled into his neck, amazed at the man in my arms. "Thank you."

We stood like that for a little while, in his kitchen, with our arms around each other. Then he asked, "Will I see you tonight?"

I pulled back and kissed his lips. "I gotta work. But I have a kickboxing lesson tomorrow night. Know of any cute instructors who are available?"

He smiled. "I'll have to check the roster. There might be someone cute..." he teased.

I grabbed his chin between my thumb and forefinger. "I only want you."

He grinned spectacularly. "You *better* only want me."

I could feel myself blush when I told him, "Just you."

"Mmm," he sighed. "You haven't blushed for me for a while. I thought I was losing my touch."

I chuckled and of course, blushed again. He leaned in and kissed me soundly. "Matt?"

"Yeah?"

"Just you too."

CHAPTER NINE

I SAW Kira at my Friday night kickboxing lesson, but then he had to work Saturday morning, so we had a late dinner at his place on Saturday night. I worked most of the next few days, and even though I saw him intermittently and spoke to him on the phone, we didn't exactly have any quality time together.

I went back to work again early on Monday morning, combing the Tomic files for anything we might have overlooked, and worked right through until Tuesday morning.

"You look like hell," Mitch greeted me cheerfully, as only he could. But he brought me coffee, so he was forgiven. "Did you pull an all-nighter?"

I nodded, and my stiff neck protested, making me groan.

He looked to the files open on my desk. "Find anything new?"

"Nah," I admitted. "But there's—"

"There's something missing," he cut me off, finishing my sentence for me.

I sighed tiredly. "You know what?" I asked, looking up at him. "The more I look, the more convinced I am."

He fell into his chair and huffed out a sigh. He stared at me for a long moment then shook his head. "Give me your notes," he said, rolling his eyes.

I grinned at my partner and slid over my notepad.

Kurt and Tony both laughed at us from their desks, and Mitch looked at them, completely resigned. "If you can't beat him…"

Ignoring their jibes at me, I explained to Mitch what I'd done. "I've cross-referenced times and locations from intel's reports against ours, and there don't seem to be any discrepancies."

Mitch looked at me curiously. "Then where's the problem?"

This was where I always lost them. "It's in his behavior."

Mitch blinked. "His behavior?"

I nodded and talked quickly so there was less time for doubt to settle in. "His actions don't add up. It's not consistent. We know he's territorial and violent. We know Homicide has him pegged for numerous disappearances but can't prove anything. We know he's capable of killing someone without rhyme or reason."

Mitch, Kurt, and Tony all stared at me.

So I continued, "But then he'll show lenience when he shouldn't. We know he has a high IQ, but at the same time, he's fucking stupid. We know he's meticulous and anal about everything to the point of OCD, but then he'll do something out of sequence. It doesn't make sense."

"So," Kurt said slowly. "You think he has a split personality?"

I exhaled loudly. "I'm not sure," I admitted.

"Maybe he's smarter than we gave him credit for," Tony said objectively. "Maybe he acted that way to make us *think* he didn't act alone? So we'd spend half our time looking for someone who doesn't exist."

I had to admit, it was a fair point. I sighed again. "Maybe."

But Mitch hadn't said a word. The three of us looked at him. He was flipping through my notes, and when he realized we were watching him, he stared at me, tapping his pen like he did when he was thinking.

"I think you're right."

I grinned at him, and Kurt and Tony groaned in unison.

Mitch shook his head. "I fucking hate it when I think you're right."

I laughed, but he was quick to his feet. "Come on," he snapped at me. "You're the one telling Berkman."

I grabbed my notepad and the files, and we headed to Berkman's office. This should be easy. The boss loved me.

The older man looked up from his computer. "You look like shit, Elliott," he barked at me. "When was the last time you slept?"

About thirty-six hours ago, but I didn't say that. Instead I told him, "I've been going through the Tomic files."

He didn't blink. He didn't move. I don't even know if he breathed.

So I told him something hadn't sat well with me this entire case. I'd pushed to look for a second operative, but without the proof, there just wasn't the time or the resources to take it further.

Berkman looked at us both. "What's changed?"

It was Mitch who answered. "My partner here has had a bee in his bonnet since day one about this, and he's gonna drive me fucking nuts until he checks this out." Then Mitch looked at me, then back to our boss and said, "And sir, he's never been wrong before."

"You agree with him?" Berkman asked him. Mitch nodded, and Berkman sighed. "What is it you're asking for?"

"We want a psych evaluation on Tomic before he goes to trial," I told him. "A full profile."

"Looking for?"

"To see if he's capable of such a diverse behavior pattern," Mitch said. "Either the man's Jekyll and Hyde, or he didn't work alone."

"You're running out of time," Berkman said, like we didn't already know.

We both nodded, and our boss pressed his lips into a thin line. "You"—he looked at me—"give the files to him." He nodded to Mitch, and I promptly handed the files over. Then he looked at Mitch. "You get the paperwork in order. I'll organize the profile. I want your reports watertight." He looked between us both like he was watching a tennis match. "Water. Tight. Do I make myself clear?"

"Yes, sir," we answered in unison and turned to leave.

"And Elliott?" he called out.

We both stopped and turned to face him, but only I answered. "Yes, sir?"

"Go home," he barked at me. "Have a sleep and a shower. You're wearing the clothes you came in here wearing yesterday, you stink, and you're no use to anyone on no sleep."

I smiled at him.

His lips curled into an almost smile. "And... good job."

"Thank you, sir."

He had his phone in his hand before we left his office. Mitch looked sideways at me before hitting me with the files I'd just handed to him. "Thanks a fucking lot," he griped. "I fucking hate it when you're right." He held up the files, shaking them at me. "I won't be going home anytime today."

I laughed at him and collected my keys from my desk on my way out. "Say hello to Anna for me."

He mocked my voice. "Say hello to Keira for me."

I got to the elevator, turned, and gave him a salute. "I will."

He flipped me the bird.

I smiled at him, but I had to admit, that was a fucking great idea. I was ridiculously tired. I'd been up for thirty-six hours straight, but I wanted to see him. I wanted to be with him, close to him.

I knew exactly what I was going to do.

I'd go to his place instead of mine. The fact he was at work and wouldn't even be there didn't bother me. I'd sleep in his bed that smelled of him.

The fact I didn't have a key was just a minor technicality.

I LOOKED up and down the hallway. It was empty, but it was habit for me to check. I took out my keys and found the one I was looking for, though it wasn't really a key at all. It was a long, flat, metal pin, the kind of key that'd open most locks on most doors. I slid the tool into the lock and jimmied it around, turning the handle until I heard a familiar click.

I slipped inside his apartment, pulling my shoes off and leaving them inside the door. His apartment was clean and quiet. The walls were bright with the sunlight streaming in, nothing out of place. It was so very... him. God, he even made his bed.

I didn't bother getting undressed. I just fell onto the soft mattress, settling into his side of the bed. It smelled of him—his shampoo, his soap, his sweat. I breathed in deeply and smiled.

With one last look at the alarm clock on the bedside table, I saw it was just after two in the afternoon. Knowing Kira wouldn't be home for at least another four hours, I closed my eyes.

I WAS BEING WATCHED. Even in my sleep, I could feel eyes on me. My skin prickled. My blood pounded in my ears. I was suddenly very aware I was not in my house—and then I remembered where I was.

I opened my eyes and saw a silhouette in the doorway.

A huge, well-defined figure with spiky black hair and dark, smiling eyes was standing in the doorway, watching me. A slow smile spread across his face as he walked toward the bed. "Do all cops know how to break and enter?"

My voice was croaky. "Only the really good ones."

He grinned. "I saw your shoes at the door," he said softly.

I smiled. "Good detective work."

"You're on my side of the bed," he said, and the mattress dipped as he put his knee on it.

"It smells like you," I told him.

He moaned softly, leaning over to press his lips to my still-sleepy eyelids. I reached out my hand, finding his forearm. "Babe, I'm all sweaty," he said.

"Mmm," I hummed. "Sweaty Kira's my favorite," I told him. He chuckled but didn't protest when I pulled him down beside me. "We can shower later."

He lay down, and I quickly settled into his side, resting

my head on his chest. He wrapped his arms around me and kissed the top of my head. "I missed you."

I gave him a squeeze. "I missed you too. I'm sorry I've worked so much this week," I told him. "I'll make it up to you."

"Hmm?" he hummed suggestively. "How do you propose to do that?"

"This weekend, I'm all yours," I promised him. "I've done enough hours to give me a weekend off."

"But that's three days away," he whined.

"Then I'll make it up to you tonight as well," I conceded, looking up at him.

He smiled and ran his fingers along my scruffy jaw. "You didn't shave."

"I didn't go home."

"You work too hard."

Ignoring his comment about my job, I rubbed my jaw along his hand. "Don't you like my scruff?"

"Mmm, I do. It suits you," he said with a smile. "But you still work too hard."

I didn't think he'd let me get away with not answering. I laid my head back down on his bare chest. "I'm a cop. It's what I do."

I could feel his chest vibrate when he chuckled. "But this weekend, you're not a cop. You'll just be my boyfriend, to do with as I see fit."

Lifting my head and resting it on my hand, I looked at him. "Now that sounds promising!"

He laughed, but then his smile died. "Oh, shit. I'm supposed to be having dinner with my parents on Saturday night."

"Oh."

"You could come with me?" He sounded unsure and hopeful at the same time.

"To your parents' house? For dinner?" I asked. "Would they mind?"

He grinned. "They like you. Of course they won't mind." He got some far-off look in his eyes as though he was concocting some sort of plan. Then he flipped me onto my back, leaned over me, and grinned. "What time will you finish on Friday?"

Suddenly a little scared by his excitement, I told him, "Well, we normally hit the gym around five-ish, I have my boxing lesson at five-thirty and then we hit the bar. Home by seven-ish." And then the loaded question, "Why? What are you planning?"

He laughed at me but leaned down and pecked his lips to mine. "If I can change dinner with Mom and Dad to Friday, then we can go camping. All weekend."

Huh? Camping? *Camping?* Was he kidding me?

He thought my expression was hilarious. I tried to explain. "I don't do camping. I don't do tents in the wilderness with wild animals. Put me in a concrete jungle with drug dealers any day." But he only laughed louder.

When he'd stopped laughing, he climbed off me. As he walked out to the living room, he told me, "I need to call Mom to see about changing our dinner plans."

"Tell her Saturday is fine," I yelled back to him. "We can stay in a fancy hotel, where there's room service and television, hot showers and flushing toilets."

He laughed again then told me from the next room to get my pretty ass out of bed and order some dinner because he was starving. I rolled my eyes. He was always starving because he exercised too damn much.

"There's no home delivery in the wilderness!" I called out. "What will you do then?"

He laughed again, but then said, "Hi, Mom... No, no, I was laughing at Matt. He's just being funny."

I was being funny?

I walked into the kitchen and pouted at him on my way past. He chuckled at me as he talked to his mom, and I could tell from this side of the conversation, dinner was now on Friday night. Which meant I was going camping.

Great.

Looking through the takeout menus, I decided on Thai for dinner. As I ordered from my cell, Kira disconnected the call to his mom and stood behind me in the kitchen. He trailed his mouth down the back of my neck down to my shoulder, with wet, open-mouthed kisses.

With dinner ordered, I put my phone on the kitchen counter but didn't turn around. Kira kept kissing all the skin his mouth could find. "This weekend will be fun. Just you and me," he said breathily in between kisses. "A secluded cabin... log fire..."

"Mm." I stretched my neck, giving him better access. "Now that kind of camping I can do."

He chuckled into my neck. "The big, brave Detective Matthew Elliott is afraid of the great outdoors?"

I turned to face him, and he was clearly amused. "Not afraid of," I clarified. "It's just out of my comfort zone."

He raised one eyebrow. "And dealing with crazed drug dealers is in your comfort zone?"

I nodded. "Yep."

He shook his head at me. "You're crazy."

"Must be if I'm considering going camping."

He laughed. But then he frowned and walked into the living room, coming back with his keys. He unthreaded one key and held it in his hand, and when he looked at me, he bit his lip.

"This is a key to my apartment," he said with a nervous smile. "You should have one. So, you know, you don't have to break in if I'm not here."

A key? A key to his apartment. *Oh, my God.*

I reached out slowly and took it. It was just a simple silver key, but what it meant wasn't simple at all. I looked up into his dark eyes and couldn't stop the grin that spread across my face. "I shouldn't really break in, you know, being a cop and all."

He chuckled and breathed out a sigh of relief. Then he shook his head. "I still can't believe you did that."

I shrugged. "I needed to see you." Then it occurred to me, I really should return the favor. "I should get you a key to my place."

He rolled his eyes. "I don't think I need one, considering I've only been there twice."

"Oh."

He lifted my chin. "But thank you for the offer." Then he kissed me, all languid and lovely, until there was a knock at the door telling us dinner had arrived.

CHAPTER TEN

WHEN I TOLD the guys at work I was going camping, they laughed for a full ten minutes. Funny bastards.

I waited until we were about to leave for the gym to tell them so there was less interrogation time, and they laughed the entire way there. When we hit the treadmills, the comments started. I should have known better than to say anything at all.

Kurt wagged his eyebrows. "Must be serious if she's getting him out of the city limits."

Tony snorted. "She's sunk her hooks in him already. Got him trained!"

Mitch grinned at me and nodded in agreement. "Oh partner, she's done a number on you already."

She. She. She.

They wouldn't believe it when I told them it wasn't a "she" at all.

It wasn't lost on me that I was now thinking *when* and not *if* I told them. Coming out to my coworkers was something I'd never dreamed I'd ever do, and there I was considering how they'd take the news, not if I told them, but when. Something I'd never dreamed I'd ever do, before Kira.

And when Mitch called out, "Hey, Frankie?" my feet lost their rhythm on the treadmill.

"Wassup?" Kira answered with a smile.

"When you spar with my partner here, would you smack some sense into him? Please?"

Kira's eyes flickered to mine, and he grinned. "I'll try, but he's pretty quick."

"Not quick enough," Kurt puffed as he ran. "The new girlfriend's quicker."

Kira's eyes lit up, and he smirked at me. "Is that so?"

I kept running, not looking directly at any of them, and particularly not at Kira. This conversation was hitting a little too close to home.

"Yeah," Tony said with a laugh. "But sshhhh! It's all a big secret."

Mitch snorted. "It's a secret because it's Keira Knightley."

Kira laughed, and I shook my head in disbelief at the conversation. Kurt reached over and slapped my shoulder. "Well, whoever it is, our boy here is in *looove.*"

And I tripped over my feet.

Fuck. Fuck. Fuck.

The guys all laughed at me, and I could feel Kira's wide, amused eyes on me, but I didn't look at him. I hit the stop button on the treadmill but didn't wait for it to slow down. I jumped off the machine and told them all, very maturely, to get fucked.

I could still hear them laughing when I walked into the boxing room.

Soon after, Kira followed me in. He didn't say anything,

just smirked as he set up the room while I strapped my hands, pretending I wasn't embarrassed.

But he stood right in front of me, and eventually I looked at him, not knowing what to expect. I couldn't deny it. The L word threw me off guard.

I'd be lying if I said it didn't scare me. Scared me, because it wasn't something I was expecting. Scared me, because I'd never been in love before. Not *real* love anyway. It really scared me because I thought what Kurt said could quite possibly, might be, just a little bit true.

Kira took my hands, pulled at and tightened the tape strapping. "So... they've been giving you hell, huh?"

I barked out a laugh. "You have no idea."

He chuckled. "Uh, yeah, I heard."

"Sorry about that," I said quietly.

He grinned. "Don't apologize."

I shook my head. "And that was just me telling them I was going camping for the weekend!" I looked at him seriously. "Imagine if I'd told them I was having dinner with your parents as well!"

Kira laughed. "You mean dinner with Keira Knightley's parents."

I groaned. "Oh, don't you start."

He laughed again, clearly amused by the whole thing. He pushed the punching bag toward me, and our boxing session started. He took what he did very seriously. And so he should. He was very good at it.

He had me on the bag, practicing jab-kick sequences, using both sides of my body. After I'd done my rounds, he sparred with me. He kept his dark eyes focused on mine, his hands protecting his chin, but he somehow still saw what I was doing with my feet.

He kept getting into my personal space. It distracted me

and limited my kicking range, which was, I presumed, the exact reason he did it. He grinned at me and tapped my face with one hand and my ribs with his other. I looked at him, asking him with my eyes what he was doing.

"I can't wait to get you alone tonight," he whispered gruffly.

And just like that, with just his words, my cock twitched.

I jumped back from him, and still bouncing on my toes, I palmed my dick.

He threw his head back and laughed, then with a spectacular smile, called our session over. He started to pack up the room, telling me he was done for the day. "Just a quick shower," he said. "Then I'm going straight home."

I found myself grinning, despite myself, as I pulled the tape off my hands. "I'm not going for drinks with the guys," I told him. He stacked the mats and turned to look at me. I bent over to pick up my towel so he got an eyeful of my ass, and when I looked back at him, I very slowly, very deliberately, raked my eyes up his body. I moaned. "Mm, yeah. I've got somewhere else I'd rather be."

His eyes grew impossibly darker, and he smiled slowly. I looked at the clock on the wall. 5:32.

I worked out roughly how long it would take me to get home, showered, and back to his place. I palmed my dick deliberately and smiled. "See you in thirty."

CHAPTER ELEVEN

AS PER HIS INSTRUCTION, I pulled into the under-cover parking lot of Kira's apartment. He met me there with a duffel bag of clothes, a box of food, and another bag of God only knew what.

"We're only going for the weekend, yes?" I asked, looking at what he'd packed.

He laughed as he got into my car. He was dressed in ordinary jeans and a shirt, but the grin he wore was something else entirely. "Yes, just the weekend."

I pulled the car out of the complex and asked, "Where to?"

"Mom and Dad live in Claremont, so onto the I-5.".

We found ourselves in the ebb and flow of traffic, and I thanked him again for being a good sport with the guys at the gym, and then I apologized again for the same.

Kira looked at me and smiled kindly. "I know they mean no harm," he said. "All jokes aside, it's obvious they respect you a lot."

I nodded. "Yeah, I guess so. Joking is how they deal."

"And as for all the secrecy," he went on to say, "we just

do what we have to do, my dear man." He reached a hand over the console and squeezed my thigh. "Whatever it takes."

He didn't move his hand, keeping it on my leg, so I slid my fingers over his. "Whatever it takes."

THE DRIVE TO HIS PARENTS' place took about forty minutes. We were far enough out of the city that I didn't fear being spotted, so I didn't hesitate to step out of the car and walk with him to the front door.

The house was an older, bungalow-style home, very suburban, very family. Kira bounced up the steps and opened the front door. He called out, "Mom?" and he just walked straight in.

He turned and smiled at me, waiting for me to follow him inside, and the first thing I noticed was the smell. Something smelled delicious.

"Oh, good," we heard his mother say from somewhere in the house. "Kira, get this down for me."

After taking our shoes off, we walked into the kitchen. Kira quickly reached up and collected a container off the top shelf and handed it to his mother along with a kiss on the cheek. His father walked in at the same time with some fresh herbs in his hand.

The conversations started between them. I was soon smiling and laughing at the antics, jokes and eye rolls between them. Sal signed to Kira when Yumi wasn't looking, and then when Sal wasn't looking, Yumi signed about her husband behind his back while Kira tried not to laugh out loud. I had no idea what they were saying to each other, but it was funny as hell to watch.

Soon enough, we were eating the most delicious dinner I think I'd ever had, while the conversation never stopped. Yumi asked me fifty questions, about work mostly, but then she asked me about my family.

"My mom passed away when I was seventeen," I told them, and the three of them stared at me. I looked directly at Kira and said, "I never knew my dad." I felt his hand on my leg under the table, and he squeezed my knee. I looked back to his parents and smiled. "I joined the police force when I was eighteen. That's the story of my life."

Yumi smiled kindly. "You must be good," she announced. "Only good cops go on the television."

I chuckled, but it was Kira who answered. "He's the best there is, Mom."

Sal signed, and I looked to Kira to translate. "He wants to know if you've ever been in a gunfight like in the movies."

I laughed. "I've been shot at, punched, kicked, threatened with knives, bats, broken bottles..."

Kira whispered, "Jesus..."

I looked at Sal and smiled. "But no John Wayne gunslinging."

Kira shook his head. "I think we need to take your kickboxing defense a little more seriously."

I grinned at him. "I thought you *were* taking it seriously."

Yumi stood up to clear the table. "Kickboxing not make him bulletproof."

"No, it won't," Kira mumbled. He looked at me seriously. "I can't believe you get shot at!"

I snorted. "I'm a narcotics cop in LA! Of course I've been shot at."

Kira blinked, seemingly stuck for words, but Yumi called him to help her in the kitchen, leaving me alone with

Sal. I looked at Kira's father, and he was smiling at his son as he walked out of the room. When he looked at me, he laughed and stood up, indicating I should follow him.

He walked into the family room and over to the fireplace. When I stood beside him, he pointed to the photographs along the mantelpiece. It was like a visual growth chart of Kira, from a black-haired, brown-eyed, smiling baby boy, to an elementary schoolboy, to a soccer-playing kid, to a karate-outfit-wearing teenager, to a graduate.

I looked at Sal and smiled. "He kept you busy?"

He laughed and nodded. He pointed to the photos of the baby and small boy and waggled his hand in a so-so manner, indicating Kira wasn't a bad kid. Then he pointed to the photos of him as a teenager and rolled his eyes.

I laughed. "I bet he was a handful as a teen." Then I looked closer at the photograph of Kira playing soccer. I looked directly to Sal so he could read my lips. "Did he have a black eye in that photo?"

Sal nodded and sighed. Then he put his hands up in the fighter's position.

I asked, "He was always fighting?"

Sal nodded and pointed to the photo of Kira in his karate garb. I nodded in understanding. "He did martial arts to learn self-defense?"

Sal nodded again, just as Kira walked back into the room. He walked right up to me and slid his arm around my waist. "Is my dad telling you embarrassing stories?"

I chuckled, a little nervous at his display of affection in front of his father. "Just that you used to fight a lot."

"Still do," he said proudly. "Just now I get paid to teach it and keep fit."

I shook my head at him, then looked back to the school-aged photos. "It's hard to believe you were ever that little," I said, rubbing my hand up Kira's back. Even knowing Sal was deaf and couldn't hear me, I leaned and whispered, "You were still cute, though."

Sal signed something, making Kira laugh. "Dad says you'll need to work on hiding your mouth when you want to talk dirty."

Oh. My. God. I forgot Sal could read lips…

I could feel my face heat, no doubt turning a dozen shades of mortified. Kira kissed the side of my head, still laughing, and a grinning Sal clapped his hand against my arm.

"Mom," Kira called out with a laugh. "We're gonna head off now." Kira swiped the keys from my pocket. I asked him what the hell he thought he was doing, and he looked at me very seriously. "Do you know where we're going?"

I sighed. "No."

Kira looked at me and grinned. Apparently, he'd won that one. I looked at Sal, and while Kira wasn't looking, he quickly pointed to the kitchen where Yumi was, then to Kira, and then he entwined his middle and forefinger. He was telling me they were close, and they were a lot like each other.

I laughed, making Kira look at me. He then looked to his father. He knew what we were doing, and apparently speaking in sign language behind each other's backs was a family trait.

Yumi came out with containers of leftovers for us to take with us and was still giving us instructions when we were walking out the door.

"Yes, Mom," Kira said for the tenth time. "I've been there a hundred times. I'm sure we'll find it just fine, even in the dark."

Sal signed something as we got into the car, and Kira snorted. When we'd pulled out onto the street, I asked what his dad had said. "He said 'have some pity on me, I live with her.'"

I laughed, and Kira looked at me, unable to help but laugh too.

"Hey, babe?" I asked.

"Yeah?"

"Your parents are good people."

WE HEADED out on Highway 2, following signs to Wrightwood. But it was dark and the lights of LA got fewer and farther between. The highway got smaller with more twists and turns as we got farther into the mountains, and the night somehow got darker.

Kira talked so easily, about his work, about my work, about his family and about mine. And I knew, although it hadn't been said, this weekend was a test for us. Maybe even make-or-break for us. I didn't know what that meant exactly, or where it left us either way.

But I was hoping like all hell we were on the "make it" side of the line come Sunday night.

As we reached the township of Wrightwood, Kira navigated through the streets easily. And when he pulled up in front of a two-story house and parked the car, I asked him why we'd stopped there.

He replied simply. "This is it."

"Here?" I asked, confused. "You said camping... in a cabin... in the wilderness." I could see lights of other houses. This was hardly the wilderness.

Kira laughed and grabbed some bags out of the car. I

followed him with my arms full, and when he unlocked the door and turned the lights on, I couldn't believe my eyes.

It was a wooden cabin all right, but it was decked out with a kitchenette, sofa, rugs, and stairs, which I presumed led to an upstairs bedroom. I mean, it was by no means extravagant, but it was homey. There was even a fireplace.

Kira smiled at my expression. "What were you expecting?"

"A wooden shack," I answered honestly. "In the wilderness."

He laughed. "This was my grandparents'," he said, putting the bags at the foot of the stairs. "It used to be a small cabin, but Mom and Dad spend a lot of time here and have done it up over the years. We used to come up here all the time when I was a kid. In the summer, I'd camp in a tent out back." He walked through, flipping on lights as he went. "We've always called it 'the cabin,' and we joke about our type of camping."

I put the box of food on the kitchen counter, taking in the room around me. The walls were a reddish timber, and there were photographs placed sporadically along them. There was a large, comfy-looking sofa, a lamp on the side table, and a small, round dining table. The windows were blackened by the night outside them, and there was something else... something that took me a little while to put my finger on...

Silence. Complete and utter silence.

"It's perfect."

Kira grinned at me. "It sure is."

We put the few food items away in the kitchen, then Kira showed me upstairs. It was an open loft-style space with timber-paneled walls, raked ceiling, a wall of curtains at one end, and a bed at the other.

"Bathroom through there," he told me, pointing to a door. "It's only small and basic."

"Considering I thought I'd need to dig a hole to use the bathroom, babe, I think this is the Hilton," I told him. "Actually, this kind of camping, I could get used to."

He laughed at me and walked toward the wall of curtains, pulling them back to reveal large glass doors. "Come on," he said, still smiling. "Take a look out here."

I followed him out onto what I realized was a balcony, only it was more like a large deck. It faced the back of the house and was shrouded in darkness. He pointed to some neighboring house lights not too far off. "See? Not complete wilderness," he said, sliding his arms around me from behind. "I didn't bring you into the *absolute* middle of nowhere."

He gave me general directions, like the way we came, where the town was, and the river. "We'll go hiking tomorrow," he hummed. "I can show you everything."

"Hiking?"

His chest vibrated as he chuckled. "Yes, Matt. Hiking."

I sighed as he rubbed his nose along the back of my neck, and his arms tightened around me. Neither of us spoke for a while, we just stood out there in the dark, his arms wrapped safely around me.

I could feel the planes of his chest against my back, his strong arms around my waist, his breath on my neck. It made me shiver.

"Are you cold?"

I shook my head. "Mm-mm," I told him, as I turned around in his arms. "Not at all." I cupped one hand along his jaw, and even in the dark night, I could see him. My eyes were drawn to his mouth, his perfect lips.

When I looked at his eyes, their intensity and the way he looked into me made my heart thump funny.

"Kira," I breathed his name, and his eyes seemed to deepen, darken.

He nodded, like he understood what I needed. He knew what I wanted, what I needed, without a word. He just knew. Without a sound, he took my hand and led me inside.

He took his sweet time with me, undressing me slowly, reverently, like I was something to be savored. And that was what he did. He savored me, every inch of skin, every touch, every kiss. He had me on my back, my legs bent up to my chest, and when he finally pushed inside me, he cradled my face and kissed me. Slowly and so completely, he thrust so sure, so deep.

He was all I could feel as he filled me again and again. He was over me, all around me, inside me. He was everywhere and everything, and it wasn't enough. His tongue filled my mouth while his cock filled my ass, and it still wasn't enough.

For all the times he'd fucked me, he'd never fucked me like this. Because this wasn't fucking.

It was in his eyes, in his touch, in his kiss. It was in his heartbeat, pulsing against my chest and inside me. It was how he moaned my name, it was how he murmured and pleaded, and it was how his fingers dug into my skin. It wasn't fucking. It was emotion and pure need.

He was making love to me.

"Oh, Kira."

He shuddered, pushing up into me. He bucked, and I could feel him swell and surge, and with the sweetest sound, he came.

My orgasm seized me from nowhere, ripping pleasure

from my bones. Wedged hard between us, my cock erupted, causing Kira to moan long and low in my ear. He set me flying and falling as he held me, grounded me.

I was lost to sensation, remotely aware of him moving me, rolling me over. I came back to Earth, back into my body, and I was sprawled face down on the bed. Every cell in my body was spent.

Kira came back from the bathroom completely naked, his long cock heavy and limp. So beautiful. He trailed kisses over my back, and with a warm, wet washcloth, he cleaned me.

"How did you end up with lube in your hair?" he asked with a chuckle.

Even half-asleep, I laughed. I had very vivid memories of him guiding his cock inside me, then grabbing the back of my neck to pull me in to kiss him. "Um, *you* would be the reason I have lube in my hair."

He chuckled and used the washcloth to wipe down my hair. Then he leaned over me and kissed the back of my neck. "Your hair curls right here when it's wet," he murmured and nudged the spot with his nose. "And here," he whispered and kissed behind my ear.

Then he kissed down my shoulder, rolling me onto my side. He pulled me against him, my back to his chest, and his arms wrapped around me protectively.

It was a blissful sleep that took me.

I WOKE up to the weirdest sound. Birds—a whole symphony of birds. I wasn't entirely sure how I could sleep through traffic and sirens at home and be woken up by birds chirping.

Or maybe it was the feeling of fingers tracing patterns on my back. Whatever it was, I woke up smiling.

"Good morning," a sleepy voice said right near my ear. I hummed my reply, and when I opened my eyes, what I saw was almost surreal.

Trees, the mountains, the valley. The view filtered through morning sunlight was amazing.

"I told you it was beautiful," Kira said beside me. "It's why I wanted you to wake up here."

I sat up in bed and scrubbed my hands over my eyes. I looked at him and smiled. He was sleep-rumpled and gorgeous. I looked back to the view outside the window, then back to him. "The view inside is better."

He chuckled and sat up beside me. "Wanna see it close up?"

My eyes trailed down his body to his crotch. I licked my lips and nodded.

He threw his head back and laughed. "I meant outside. The mountains. I thought we could go for a run before breakfast."

I fell back against the pillows with a groan. "I like my idea much better."

But fifteen minutes later, I was following him down a well-worn track through the trees. While I could run for miles on a treadmill, running over open terrain was something else entirely, and it was out here that I got to see just how fit Kira was.

We snaked our way along the trails, and if it weren't for the occasional passing jogger or walkers, I'd have thought we were lost. The people we passed nodded and smiled, and there were even a few cheerful "good mornings."

No one knew me here, no one recognized me. I loved

the anonymity, the freedom. I could do what I liked. I could go jogging with my boyfriend. I could be the *real* me.

I was grinning when I stopped to catch my breath along a break in the path. Kira stopped ahead of me and jogged back to where I was. He pulled my cap off my head and grinned. "Out of shape, Detective."

I scoffed at him. "I'm in good shape, just not as fit as the fitness instructor."

He put my LA Lakers cap on his head and grinned at me. "Main part of town is about a quarter mile farther along this track," he said, starting to jog the way he pointed. He was a good forty yards ahead of me, and he called out, "There's a coffee shop!"

Magic words, those. Of course I beat him there.

We took a moment to catch our breaths, then took our coffees to go and strolled the main street. It was a scenic little town, and Kira told me what he knew and what he remembered from coming here as a kid.

We took our time. We just walked and talked. We didn't hold hands or anything, but it was still the first time I'd been out in public with him. I liked it.

When it was time to head back, I started off walking toward the trail, not looking forward to the return uphill run. But Kira stopped me. "We'll go this way," he said, nodding toward the road.

"Why?"

"Because the house is just up here," he said, laughing at my expression.

"You mean to tell me, you made me run all that way through the trees when I could have just walked two blocks for coffee?" I glared at him for good measure, but he just laughed at me, so I told him, "You're not keeping my Lakers cap."

He grinned so goddamn beautifully. "Yes, I am," he said, pulling it tighter onto his head. "It's mine now."

"Is that so?"

"I'd like to see you get it off me." He grinned again, wagging his eyebrows at me, taunting me.

He took off running up the sidewalk, laughing. He beat me back to the house easily and declared the cap was now rightfully his.

But it wasn't until later when he dropped to his knees and took me into his mouth, wearing nothing but the cap, that I told him he could have it.

I turned the cap around so it faced the back. I needed to see his face, his eyes, his lips as he sucked and swallowed. He took my length into his throat, sucking the orgasm from deep in my belly, and I told him it was his.

The cap. Me. Whatever he wanted. It was his.

CHAPTER TWELVE

I SOON FOUND out what the extra bag Kira had brought was for when we spent the afternoon hiking, much to my dismay. I swore to him I'd hate it and he'd have to carry my ass home, but the truth was I loved it. I had the best afternoon. We took the trail for high-fitness hikers, which should have been a fair warning to how difficult it would be.

It was hard going. The mountain had a rocky terrain, some of it steep, none of it easy, but we followed the ridgeline and finally descended to the river. It could have been a million miles from civilization, it was so secluded. The summer sun wasn't so hot in the mountains, but after the hike, we were both sweating and the river was just too inviting.

Kira just stripped off—no hesitation, no fear—and I followed in behind him. We spent about an hour there, swimming and sunbathing without a stitch of clothing on. It was the most liberating thing I'd ever done.

We lay on the large boulder by the edge of the water, staring at the sky, sunning ourselves dry. We didn't speak, but it was a peaceful silence. Kira reached out his hand, looking for mine, and when I gave it to him, he threaded our fingers. After a long while, like he could read my exact thoughts, he said, "This sure beats the grime and crime of LA."

I turned my head to look at him, giving him a lazy smile. "It sure does."

He smiled back at me, lifted our joined hands to his mouth, and kissed my knuckles. "We better get going," he told me. He jumped to his feet with more energy than should be possible, and pulled me up.

We got dressed, and as Kira turned to lead the way out, I grabbed his hand. "Wait."

He looked at me, alarmed. "What is it?"

"I just wanted to say thanks," I admitted, a little embarrassed.

"What for?"

"For this." I waved my hand at the river, the trees. "I would have lived my whole life without doing something like this if it weren't for you."

He smiled. "Then we shall have to do it again sometime."

I grinned. "Really?"

"Absolutely."

He stepped closer to me, held my face, and kissed me breathless. And despite having to walk back up that fucking mountain, I grinned all the way home.

WHEN WE GOT BACK, we were both starving and exhausted, and by the time I got out of the shower, Kira had started cooking dinner. So while he worked his magic in the kitchen, I fixed the fire, pulled the sofa bed out, and brought down some blankets.

Kira looked at me questioningly, so I told him, "I thought we could spend tonight down here."

"Why, Matthew Elliott," he said with a smirk. "Do you suggest a romantic night in front of the fire?"

I walked into the kitchen and squeezed his ass. "There's that, Kira Takeo Franco," I returned the full name favor. "And the fact I'll be too tired to make it up those stairs later on."

He chuckled, bumped his hip to mine, and kissed my cheek. "If hiking was too much, then I better take it easy on you tonight."

"You better not," I told him.

"If you insist," he smirked. Then he ran his nose along my freshly showered neck. "You smell so good."

And right on cue, ruining the moment, my stomach growled really loudly.

Kira laughed. "Dinner smells good too, apparently."

It was a noodle stir-fry of some description, and it tasted even better than it smelled. After we'd eaten, we fell onto the sofa bed. I stripped down to my underwear, snuggled into his side, and tried to watch the Saturday night game.

But I was so tired after the day hiking. I tried to stay awake, but my blinks kept getting longer. I remembered watching the Steelers being down two at the second quarter, I remembered Kira pulling the blanket over us, him kissing the side of my head, telling me to "go to sleep, baby," and the very last thing I remembered was thinking that was a really good idea.

"OW!" I yelled into my pillow. "You bit me!"

His whole body vibrated as he laughed.

I couldn't believe he just did that. "I said you can *kiss* my ass! I didn't say *bite* it!"

"Well, come running with me," he said again, still laughing.

"No," I groaned, trying to snuggle into the mattress. "It's our last day here. Let's stay in bed."

He nipped his teeth into the flesh of my ass again, then licked me. "You're insatiable."

I lifted my ass for him, hoping he'd lick me again. But he didn't. He slapped me, right on my backside. "Get this beautiful piece of ass out of bed," he said with a laugh, rolling off the mattress.

I groaned, rubbing my ass. "Is that all I am to you? A piece of ass?"

I meant it as a joke, but Kira certainly didn't smile. He looked a little startled, and a little offended. He shook his head and whispered, "No..."

I smiled at him, trying to put the humor back into the conversation, got up, and stretched. "I'll go running," I told him, walking to the stairs. "But only because it's with you."

When I looked back at him as I trudged up the stairs, I saw the slow smile spread across his face. He was still smiling when I came back downstairs, only this time he grinned at me from under my Lakers cap.

I meant *his* Lakers cap.

"Nice hat," I deadpanned as we headed out the door.

"You like it?" he asked with a grin. "I just got it yesterday."

I rolled my eyes at him and started out running ahead of him. He caught up easily, and we ran in a comfortable silence, just the sounds of our footfalls as we took the now familiar track. I might have complained about it, but I could see why he loved running—the fresh air, the forest.

"I can see why you enjoy it," I told him as we near the end of the track. He looked at me questioningly, so I explained, "Running through the national park. It's pretty."

"It is," he agreed. "But that's not why."

I stopped running and tried to not look so out of breath. "Then why?"

"Because we can do this here, we can run together here. Out in the open," he said with a shrug. "It's not like we can be seen together at home."

Oh.

"Oh." It was about all I could say. "I'm sorry, I..."

"Hey," he said with a smile, stepping in front of me. "It's just the way it is, for both of us, not just you." He put his fingertips under my chin and lifted my face. "And I could never do this at home," he said as he kissed me softly on the lips.

He smiled and rubbed his thumb along my chin. He looked into my eyes as though he wanted to say something else, but he didn't.

"What is it?" I prompted him.

He shook his head and huffed with a smile. "Nothing."

We grabbed coffee and walked back to the house. He was quiet, not sullen, but more reflective. He wasn't his usual smiling, laughing, smartass self. I asked him what was wrong, but he dismissed me, telling me everything was great.

I tried not to let it bother me, because it was kind of obvious something wasn't right, but I figured he'd tell me when he was ready.

We showered together and gave mutual, soapy hand jobs. His orgasm beckoned my own, and with the water streaming over both us, Kira kept his forehead on mine. His eyes were deep and dark, and I wondered what he saw when he looked at me. Because he stared at me, his eyes drilled into mine, and his mouth opened like he was trying to say something, but his eyes closed and he kissed me instead.

It was a different kind of kiss, deep and consuming. His fingers threaded through my hair, around my neck, my jaw. He was devouring me with his lips, his tongue, and his holding-too-tight hands, and my just-spent cock throbbed and twitched against his.

He broke the kiss so he could smile. He looked down to my dick. "You are insatiable."

The seriousness of the moment was over, and I chuckled. "It's your fault."

I turned the water off, and he handed me a towel, declaring it was time for food. After we were dressed, I stood next to him in the kitchen, and we talked while he made us an early lunch.

"I don't want to leave," I admitted. "I thought I would have some wilderness weekend in a tent somewhere. But it wasn't like Grizzly Adams at all."

Kira laughed. "Grizzly Adams? Is that what you thought?" I nodded, and he shook his head at me. He handed me a plate with a sandwich and salad, and he smiled kind of sadly. "I don't want to leave either."

"Can we come back?" I asked.

"Sure can." He nodded with a smile. "Next time we have time off together." And I felt better already, knowing it wouldn't be our last time here.

We ate our lunch, and he told me about how his parents came up here every chance they got. He told me his dad always joked about how peaceful it was here.

I nodded, agreeing completely, and Kira blinked. "Uh, Matt?" he said flatly. "Dad's deaf. He can't hear how peaceful it is. It was a joke."

I laughed at myself for missing the joke completely, and Kira rolled his eyes. As we tidied up after lunch, I asked, "So you've always known sign language?"

Kira nodded. "Since I could talk. I learned to talk and sign like it was no big deal. I didn't know any different."

"Would you teach me?" I asked, and Kira stopped and stared at me. So I quickly explained, "I'd just like to be able to do it, you know, so I can try and keep up with conversations with your parents."

For a few long seconds, Kira just stared at me. He blinked and nodded slowly and then looked at me in a way that made me nervous. Not nervous in a bad way, but nervous in a heart-thumping-funny kind of way.

He crossed the kitchen floor and pecked my lips with his. "Thank you." He said it so quietly I almost didn't hear him.

He was thanking me? "What for?"

"For asking to learn. For wanting to know," he answered. "Some people just ignore my dad and exclude him because he can't hear."

I shrugged. "Well, it's their loss. I like your dad. He's funny." Then I smiled at him. "Plus, I'd like to know what you three say about me behind my back."

He laughed, grinning hugely as he showed me the basics, folding my fingers accordingly—hello, goodbye, please, sorry, and thank you. I practiced, and he kissed me softly. "You don't have to do this, you know," he said quietly.

"I know," I told him. "I want to."

He took my right hand, and he stared at it for a long moment. He swallowed thickly, and just as I was about to ask what was wrong, he folded my fingers down. He straightened out my thumb, forefinger and little finger, but the other two were still folded against my palm.

He wouldn't look at me. He was just staring at my hand, but I could see his chest rise and fall as his breath quickened.

I looked down at my hand. He'd formed it that way deliberately. "Kira, what does this mean?"

He was still staring at my hand, but he whispered the words so quietly it took me a second to register what he said.

"I love you."

I love you...

My head jerked up to look at his face instead of my hand, but then he covered my fingers with his, like he was trying to hide his words.

My heart was thumping against my ribs, my stomach was knotted, and I couldn't seem to speak. He finally looked at me. His dark eyes were afraid and hopeful, and his voice was quiet. "Before we came here, I thought you were too good to be true." He shook his head, "I thought this weekend I would see some part of you that didn't make you so perfect, something that I didn't like, but there's nothing. You're just everything I could ask for." He was rambling. "Coming here with you only sealed what I already knew. I'm falling in love with you. I know we've only been together for six weeks, and it's too soon, but I... I... I just wanted you to know, and I don't expect you to say it back."

I pulled my hand out from under his, and keeping my fingers like he showed me, I held my hand up, palm facing him. Without saying a word, I told him I loved him too.

He looked at my hand, then into my eyes, and the smile he gave me was fucking beautiful.

His eyes were wide and questioning, almost disbelieving. So I gave him a nod, and he laughed with relief. Then he held my face, and he crushed his mouth to mine. He opened his mouth wide, twirling his tongue with mine as he held me.

Right there in the kitchen, we kissed. It was so deep, slow and consuming, I thought he was trying to crawl inside me. Although our desire grew—I could feel him harden against me—we didn't move to undress.

It was more than raw passion. So much more.

It was emotion. And when we broke apart to breathe, Kira kept my face against his, our mouths against each other, and as his eyes slowly opened, I could see it.

It was love.

I smiled, and he smiled. When I blushed, he laughed. I put my finger to his lips, but he still smiled. "Do you mean it?" he asked. "Is that how you really feel about me?"

I nodded. "I'm new to the whole love thing," I admitted quietly.

Kira pressed his hand to my chest. "But I make your heart beat funny?"

I nodded.

Then he slid his hand to my stomach. "You get butterflies when you think of me?"

I chuckled and nodded.

He smiled, and he traced my temple with his fingers. "Do you think of me all the time?"

All the damn time. I nodded. Then he whispered, "Do you dream of me?"

I smiled and nodded, embarrassed to admit that.

He lifted my chin with his fingers, and his eyes were so

close to mine. "Does the thought of not seeing me make you feel sick? Is it confusing and disorienting and frightening and wonderful?"

I looked into his eyes and nodded quickly.

Kira smiled and kissed me chastely. "I love you too."

CHAPTER THIRTEEN

I GOT to work early on Monday, figuring with the weekend away, I'd have emails and messages to get through. I wasn't disappointed.

My mind kept wandering. I couldn't help but think of him—how we'd packed up the cabin, made out some more, then driven back to the city. We'd stopped in to see his parents and handed back the keys to the cabin. We'd stayed for a cup of coffee before we went back to his place, and I had sworn his parents had noticed the difference between us.

I felt like it was glaringly obvious. We were in love. I loved him. He loved me. I felt like it was written in flashing neon signs, and I couldn't stop fucking smiling.

I was still grinning like an idiot when the others got to the office. They were full of snide remarks and knowing looks, and like always, I ignored them, not answering any of their questions about my weekend. Kurt and Tony were relentless until Mitch sat down in his chair across from me. "Leave him alone, guys. He's in love, remember?"

Just the mention of the word love gave me away. I smiled and blushed like a schoolgirl.

"Holy shit," Mitch whispered. I looked at him as he leaned back in his chair. His eyes didn't leave my face. He shook his head and muttered, "Well, I'll be damned. You went and fell in love."

I looked at him, trying to control my grin, and changed the topic completely. "Any developments over the weekend I should know about?"

He was still staring at me. "A lot, apparently."

I rolled my eyes at him. "I meant work-related."

He grinned. "Nothing we couldn't handle." Then he added with a flicker of his eyebrows, "How about you? Anything you couldn't handle?"

I cleared my throat and smiled. "I managed just fine, thank you."

Mitch nodded. "I bet you did."

Kurt and Tony both laughed, finding my newfound love life amusing. But they soon got called away, and when it was just Mitch and me, I took a deep breath, and before I lost my nerve, I said, "I need to talk to you later. Just us, okay?"

Mitch blinked, surprised. "Sure." He looked around the office, and while there were one or two others at their desks not paying any attention to us, we were basically alone. "Don't want to talk about it now?"

I didn't want to have my coming-out discussion at work. "Not here," I told him, suddenly very nervous about what it was I'd be telling him. "It's important."

Mitch grinned. "You're not getting married, are you?"

I laughed. "No."

"That's a shame," he joked. "Because I'd make an

awesome best man." I laughed at him, but then his eyes grew wide. "She's not pregnant, is she?"

I snorted at the likelihood of that. "Uh, no."

"Elliott! Seaton!" Berkman, yelled across the office. "My office. Now!"

Whenever the boss hollered, we didn't waste time. Both Mitch and I quickly followed him into his office, where an older woman was waiting. We were introduced to Doctor Helen Goldstein, and Berkman told us the profile on Tomic had been done. I was a little confused as to why the profiler was here and not just a file of her findings.

"You're both wondering what I'm doing here," Helen said, more of a statement than a question. "Commander Berkman thought it best if you heard it from me directly."

She had our undivided attention. Mitch and I didn't say a word.

Doctor Goldstein took a deep breath and started. "I spent all last week reading files and reports, watching footage and interviews. I even met with Mr. Tomic twice, under guarded supervision, of course."

She paused for effect, so I jumped in, asking, "What did you find?"

She didn't answer me directly. "Detective Elliott, you said you believed something doesn't add up, as though Tomic's character is contradictory."

I nodded. "Yes."

The doctor nodded slowly. "I agree." Then she looked between Mitch and me. I guessed Berkman had heard this already. "On paper, from the research I've done, Tomic is dominant and sadistic, cold and cruel. He has no conscience."

I nodded. We knew this.

She looked at our boss before turning back to us. "The

man sitting in that jail cell awaiting trial is not. He is unassuming and submissive by nature."

A cold shiver ran the length of my spine. Then she said what I both dreaded and expected to hear.

"I don't believe it's the same man."

"Could he just be psycho?" Mitch asked bluntly.

"If you mean does he have Dissociative Identity Disorder," she said clinically, "I can't be sure without further observation, but I'm inclined to say no. He does not."

"It's been two different people all along," I said out loud. "I knew the bastard didn't work alone."

Mitch sighed. "But there's only been one guy identified, partial fingerprints, and one match of DNA." He looked at me. "Matt, I'm not disagreeing. I just don't understand."

"It's okay," I replied. "Neither do I."

Berkman clapped his hands together, making us look at him. "Then pull the case apart. Once, twice, three times if you have to, until you do understand."

Doctor Goldstein left, Kurt and Tony were pulled off the new case, and the Tomic file was officially back to priority one. We were on a deadline. Court proceedings started in two weeks.

Needless to say, I was not exactly popular with the boys.

We spent the next week re-doing work we'd already done, and my request for a private conversation with Mitch —my coming-out conversation—was long forgotten.

I saw Kira every night, though sometimes I didn't get to his house until well after midnight. After using the key he gave me, I'd crawl into bed with him, and even in his sleep, he wrapped himself around me.

Even with the hectic schedule, I kept my boxing appointments with my favorite trainer before I showered and headed back to work. I changed my half-hour sessions to full-hour sessions just so I could spend more time with him. Yes, the physical outlet was good for stress, but it was also like an hour of foreplay. It was physical, close contact, and we were both sweating and panting. And hard.

On Friday after our session, Kira unstrapped my hands and eyed my cock. Leaning in, he whispered, "Don't you dare jerk off in the shower. That load is mine."

I damn near came right there.

He laughed, and I went back to work with an aching dick. I told the boys my sessions were longer because I'd started kickboxing on top of my usual boxing, and they didn't even blink an eyelid. Instead, they told me I was a sucker for punishment and couldn't believe I paid good money to get beaten up.

Still, they never suspected a thing.

I wanted to tell Mitch. I wanted to share it with him, but we were tired and stressed after such a busy week, and I didn't need to blindside him with news of just who Kira was.

The next week wasn't much better. Not only was the case sucking up all my time, it was always on my mind.

On Thursday, after not seeing Kira in what felt like forever, I got to his place a little after eight with Chinese food and apologies.

"You don't have to keep saying sorry," Kira told me. "I know you didn't become one of the best cops in LA without long hours." But the disappointment on his face betrayed him.

"I'm sorry, babe," I said again, but he kissed me quiet, pressing his warm, soft lips to mine.

Then I told him I wouldn't see him all weekend, and I watched his face fall.

"See?" I cried. "This is what I meant when I told you my job is hard on relationships!" I was scared of what this meant and exactly where this conversation might go.

"Hey," he said, holding my face. "It's not the hours that bother me." Then he admitted, "It's the psychopathic drug dealers you hunt down that bother me."

"Oh."

He smiled sadly. "I just worry, that's all."

This time I kissed him quiet before I smiled and told him, "That's why I have the awesome kickboxing trainer."

He didn't smile at my joke, so I swept the hair off his forehead and reassured him. "Kira, baby, please don't worry. I'll be fine."

Looking down between us, he asked, "Do I even want to know what psycho you're chasing down this weekend?"

I didn't want to worry him, so I shook my head. "No."

He fisted my shirt and pressed his forehead to mine. His eyes slowly closed, fanning his dark lashes across his cheeks.

A sudden need came over me. I needed him. I needed him to have me.

I pulled him against me, relishing the feel of his body, his heat. I breathed in his scent, and when I kissed down his neck, I could taste him on my tongue. But I needed to taste more. So I took his face in my hands, kissing him for all I was worth.

He understood. He always did. Because he knew just what I wanted, what I needed: he took me to bed, whispering how much he loved me. And he made me his.

Twice.

MITCH and I waited until Friday night before we headed back to the docks to find Ferret.

He was there, skittish and as high as a kite. He told us Tomic's men had been around and how the drug cartel was still in order. "In fact," he said, looking around nervously, "it's stronger than ever."

We reminded him again that Tomic was still behind bars. Ferret blinked, scrubbed his hands over his face, and rambled on about keeping track of days, but he could have sworn he saw him just last week.

"That's what you told us last time," Mitch told him.

Ferret blinked again. "When did I see you?" Then the little guy twitched and shook his head. "He's gone underground," he mumbled. "Something's about to go down." He rambled on about how there was a new shipment about to hit the street and about Tomic's men, his henchmen. They were more violent and unrestrained than ever and people were disappearing.

I sighed. It seemed Ferret was a lost cause. I paid him his money for his trouble but doubted we'd be calling in to see him again. As we left, Ferret scurried out before us as always. Mitch shook his head at me, silently telling me our snitch was a lost cause, and I nodded. As we headed out along the side of the dock, we saw two men confront Ferret, grabbing him.

"Been blabbing again?" the first guy asked.

"Did you rat us out, Ferret?" the second guy said.

The men were a fair size, street tough, with cold, hard eyes, and Ferret squirmed in their grasp, denying blabbing about anything. "I didn't rat on anyone, I swear."

We couldn't just leave him outnumbered. "Gentlemen," I interrupted.

The two men looked at me, and they both smiled. They

didn't have to say, but it was obvious they knew we were cops. The second guy, who had tattoos up his neck, tightened his hold on Ferret in one hand, and the first guy, ever so casually, pulled a gun from his waistband and held it against Ferret's head.

Mitch and I had our guns drawn on instinct. Ferret paled, but his eyes were wide with fear.

"Let him go," Mitch said coolly.

"Penalty for snitching is lead injection," Tattoo Guy sneered.

"If you shoot him, we'll have to shoot you," I said with a shrug. "I'd rather not do that."

"Yeah," Mitch added. "The paperwork's a bitch."

The two men stared at us. We couldn't do anything. If one of us fired, two or more of us died. We knew it. So did they.

The second guy smirked. "Let him go," he said to Tattoo Guy. "If we shoot them now, it'll ruin all the boss's fun."

Boss?

"Who's your boss?" I asked.

"And what's his 'fun' plan?" Mitch added.

The two men sneered at us. "You'll find out soon enough." The second guy smiled menacingly. He thumbed the safety on his gun and slipped it into the waistband of his jeans. Tattoo Guy pushed Ferret to the ground at our feet, though we didn't watch our snitch scamper away. We watched the two thugs, who smiled and slipped into the darkness.

Mitch and I walked back to the car in silence, and after we'd gone a few blocks, Mitch growled. "Fuck!"

I looked at him. "You okay?"

He nodded, then looked at me with wide eyes. "Thought he was gonna shoot you."

"Nah," I played it down. "I'm quicker than him."

Mitch was quiet for a while. "What do you think he meant about his 'boss's fun'?"

I looked from the road to him and back to the road before answering quietly. "I don't know."

"Do you get the feeling we're running out of time?"

I tried not to look too worried, but I nodded. "Yeah, I do."

He nodded back. "Yeah. Me too."

WE GOT BACK TO HQ, filled in reports and gave descriptions of the two goons on the wharf and a full account of what had happened. It was after two in the morning when I let myself into Kira's.

I took my shoes off at the door, threw my jeans and shirt onto his bedroom floor, and crawled into bed. I slid in against him, fitting protectively into his side, under his arm. When I closed my eyes and could see a gun pointed at me point blank, I snuggled in a little closer.

I'd never had something to live for before. I'd never had something to lose.

"Mm, you okay?" Kira's sleepy voice croaked.

"I am now."

He squeezed me and mumbled something I couldn't understand, and his breathing lulled me to sleep.

I WOKE UP ALONE. It wasn't too unusual. Kira worked Saturday mornings, so I stretched out onto his side of the bed for a while and breathed in his smell. It made me smile.

I showered and shaved, thinking how my life with Kira in it was pretty damn great. I even shook my head at my smiling reflection. No wonder the guys at work knew something was up with me. I was smiling all the damn time.

But then I walked into the kitchen.

The *LA Times* was on the kitchen counter, opened to page two with the heading "Close Call." There was a photo of the dock and inserted file pictures of me and Mitch. The story went on to say two of the city's Fab Four were involved in an altercation with armed drug runners in an abandoned warehouse on the docks, how we were without backup and lucky to escape with our lives.

How the hell the media got hold of stories so soon I could only guess, but when I read in the second paragraph how we were chased down and shot at, I pushed the paper away and rolled my eyes.

I made myself a cup of coffee, and the longer I stared at the newspaper, the more I wondered why Kira had left it open for me. I'd been in the paper before and on TV, and it had never bothered him.

I grabbed my phone and typed out a quick message asking if I'd see him that night. I knew he was at work and would reply when he could, so I threw on one of his shirts and headed to work.

When my phone beeped with a message before lunch and his name flashed on the screen, I smiled. I was expecting a usual smart but sexy message, but his curt question threw me off guard.

SO IS IT TRUE?

I TYPED OUT MY RESPONSE.

IS WHAT TRUE?

HIS RESPONSE TOOK a minute to come through.

WERE YOU SHOT AT? Did you nearly die last night?

I REMEMBERED HAVING the gun pointed at me. Fuck. He was upset with me. Goddammit.

I picked up my phone and hit call, but it just rang. Great. Now he was ignoring me. So I texted him again.

CAN we talk about this tonight?

HIS REPLY WAS short and blunt.

SORRY, have to work.

I CONSIDERED TEXTING BACK but didn't really want to have this conversation via text. So I phoned the gym. It wasn't too uncommon for me to phone to change appointments or reschedule, so when Chris answered my call, he'd think nothing of it.

"You looking for a kickboxing appointment tonight?" he asked.

"Why's that?" I hedged.

"Frankie's closing up for me. He's got some appointments free later."

"Um..." I considered saying no, but it might be the only chance I got to see him. "Sure. Book me in for his last appointment."

"Okay, Matt," he said. "He'll see you at seven."

So just before seven, I called it a day. I headed straight to the gym, whereas the other guys opted to go straight home. I walked into the gym and almost ran into Chris. "I thought you had somewhere to be?" I joked.

He smiled. "On my way now," he said, looking at his watch. "Anniversary dinner," he explained. He looked back at Kira, who was just finishing up with a female officer. "Frankie offered to close up for me so I could leave early. Said he was only gonna get stood up anyway."

I looked at Kira. He was looking at me, and I knew he could hear our conversation. "Is that right?"

"Apparently," Chris said beside me. Then he said quietly, "He's been pissed off all day, so you'll wanna be on your toes tonight," he said with a nod toward the boxing room with a laugh. "Good luck."

"Yeah, thanks," I mumbled.

Walking in, I threw my towel over the rail on a treadmill and started my usual five-mile run. I watched the woman talking to Kira, flirting with him shamelessly. He smiled at her, and she giggled. When she touched his arm, his eyes darted to me, but he smiled for her and laughed at whatever jokes she made.

I knew what he was doing. He wanted me to see. He wanted me to watch; he wanted me to be jealous. He wanted to hurt me because I'd hurt him.

Well, two could play that game. Without stopping my run, I took off my shirt and wiped down my face and chest. Kira watched me. I could see his jaw clench, then he looked back at the woman. She giggled some more and tried to flirt seductively, so he gave her an eye-sparkling grin. I pretended to clear my throat. Some other guy called Kira over so the woman finally went on her way, and when he was done helping them both, he filled out some paperwork.

He still hadn't spoken to me.

I didn't know if it was because I was so tired or if it was because my mind was fried or if it was because Kira's anger had left a heavy ache in my chest, but the miles were hard. I could normally do five miles with no worries, but not tonight. I was barely past three when the other cops left for the night, leaving the entire gym empty except for Kira and me. I hit the stop button, slowing to a walk.

Kira leaned against the service counter watching me, and with every minute of his silence, it got harder to breathe. Then he walked to the front door, and I heard the locks click into place. The treadmill had stopped, but I was still out of breath. He just watched me struggle, and still without a word, he walked into the boxing room.

I followed him, and only after he turned to look at me for a long, drawn-out moment did he speak. "Are you okay?"

I nodded, but fear and dread that he was about to tell me we were over were lumped in my stomach. "Kira, please—"

"Was the newspaper right?" he cut me off. "Was it you?"

"I was there," I told him with a nod.

His eyes flashed. "So how close was it?"

"They pointed a gun at us," I told him honestly. "But no shots were fired. The media always exaggerates."

"Exaggerates!" he cried, and his tone surprised me. "Jesus, Matt!" He threw his hands up and turned away, pacing.

"Kira, please..."

"No, Matt. No," he spat out. He was so fucking mad. I was certain he was about to tell me we were over—and it paralyzed me. I stood there at his mercy, waiting for his words to wound me. "So is that how I'll find out?" His jaw was clenched, his tone softening as his anger gave way to hurt. "Am I gonna wonder why you don't turn up one night or don't answer your phone? Will I read about you getting shot or stabbed? Or will I see it on the six o'clock news?"

My mouth opened. I tried to speak, but I couldn't make the sounds. I wasn't even sure what I'd say if I could.

He swallowed thickly. "So if you don't come home one night, do I assume the worst? Am I gonna read about the man I love being gunned down on some derelict dock in the morning paper?"

"I'm sorry," I told him, though it sounded hugely inadequate. Even to me. "Baby, what can I do? You name it, I'll do it. Just please don't leave me."

He blinked, and his mouth fell open. "What?"

"I just found you," I blurted out, not making a great deal of sense. "I'm not sure what I'd do if I lost you."

He stood in the middle of the room as open and vulnerable as me. "Then you know exactly how I felt this morning when I read about you in the paper."

I nodded. "I'm sorry."

"Don't apologize," he said quietly.

"What else can I do?" I asked again. "Tell me."

"Talk to me!" he said with his hand to his chest. "So at least I know where you'll be."

"There is stuff I can't tell you," I told him, exasperated. "I'm not allowed to tell you, and you wouldn't want to know half of it. I know you worry about the psycho drug dealers out there." I pulled at my hair in frustration. "And they *are* psycho, Kira. They'd sooner shoot me than talk to me. I don't like it any more than you, but it's my job. It's what I do."

I walked up to him and took his hand. "I understand what you're saying... and you're absolutely right." I looked at him so he could see the seriousness in my eyes. If something were to happen to me, he shouldn't have to read about it in the morning paper. "I need to tell Mitch about us."

His brow creased, and his shoulders fell. "Matt—"

"Babe, I want to tell him. I want to tell someone how happy I am. Not only that," I told him quietly, "but if something were to happen to me, Mitch could tell you. You wouldn't need to read about it in the paper or see it on the news."

He sighed and gave me a small smile. "Did you honestly think I was going to break up with you?"

I huffed out a breath. "Yes. It scared the shit out of me."

He slid his hands around my jaw, and right there in the middle of the boxing room, he kissed me. When his lips stilled, he rested his forehead on mine. "Did you honestly think taking your shirt off on the treadmill, showing me your hot and sweaty torso, would distract me?"

I smiled. "Did it work?"

He grinned. "Maybe."

I pecked my lips to his again. Then a thought occurred to me, and I looked around. "Um, are there security cameras in here?"

Kira laughed. "No, not in here. In the main gym floor there is. Why, did you think we could give Chris some *interesting* footage?" he joked suggestively, all seriousness gone.

I chuckled at the thought of what we could do on the floor mats. "Maybe another time."

Kira's eyebrows shot up. "Did you actually want your kickboxing lesson?"

I laughed, shaking my head. "No. I want you to take me home."

"Now that I can do," he said.

When we got back to his place, we barely made it to the couch. I sheathed him in a condom and lube, then straddled him, rubbing shamelessly against his hard-on while I kissed every inch of skin I could reach.

"I need you," I told him as I licked the shell of his ear. "I need you now."

"You're not ready," he panted.

I shook my head. "Now. I need to feel you. In two days' time, I still want to be able to feel you."

He gasped in my ear, and his whole body shuddered as I impaled myself on him. It stung and burned as his thick cock stretched me, filled me, centered me. There was nothing else but me and him. It was exactly what I needed.

CHAPTER FOURTEEN

THE NEXT MORNING, Kira ate his usual mix of health grains, fruit, and yogurt as I sipped my coffee standing at the kitchen counter. I took out my phone and pressed Mitch's number. It went straight to voicemail, so I told him I needed to catch up with him. I had something to tell him, but not over the phone.

When I disconnected the call, Kira walked up behind me and kissed the back of my neck. I turned to face him, kissed his lips and, taking his hand, led him to the sofa. "You wanted to know about the type of bad guys we track down," I said, and he nodded, a little unsure. "First of all, Kira, you have to understand what I'm about to tell you could get me into trouble. It could jeopardize the case or I could be fired—"

"I don't want you to lose your job!" Kira countered quickly, alarmed.

"And I don't want to lose you," I replied simply. "I love my job, I do. But I love you too, and I trust you. I *know* I can trust you, I can feel it in my bones. I've never broken protocol before," I told him honestly, "but I've never had a reason to. I want to tell you this, not just so you understand, but because I want to prove to you how much you mean to me."

Kira squeezed my hand and nodded.

So even though I shouldn't, I took a deep breath and told him everything I knew about Pavao Tomic. I told him of the crimes he was accused of, how we'd tracked him for months, how we had witnesses, surveillance, intel, and that we even had DNA. But even though every shred of evidence we had pointed to Tomic and Tomic alone, I wasn't sold.

I told him how I'd spent hours going through reports and case files, finally convincing Mitch that Tomic couldn't have worked alone. I just knew it, and as cliché as it sounded, my gut instinct was never wrong.

I explained how the profiler had agreed with me and how Berkman had ordered the case reopened. We were on a deadline because the court case started next week, and we needed this watertight or the bastard could walk.

"What makes you so unsure?" Kira asked thoughtfully. "What makes you doubt the evidence?"

I ran my hands through my hair. "Something I can't put my finger on. Like how one personality trait contradicts the other, how it's like he's two people in one. Like somehow he can be in two places at once."

Kira nodded. "Like he has a twin."

It was a moment of absolute clarity, as though a light was switched on over my head. My heart stopped, and I could feel the realization trickle down my spine. "Oh my God. It's *exactly* like he has a twin."

I jumped to my feet, and one second later, I was on the phone to HQ demanding information be sought from the

Croatian consulate on all known relatives and birth records of Pavao Tomic.

They told me they'd phone me right back, so I hit Mitch's number again. When it went straight to voicemail, the only thing I said was, "Call me. Now."

Kira was looking at me, a little bewildered. So I grabbed his face and kissed him. "You're a genius." I couldn't help but laugh. "Of course he has a twin. It makes perfect sense." I shook my head, still trying to get my head around it. "I can't believe I never saw that!" I cried, running my free hand through my hair. "For months we've followed him, watched his every move. We only ever saw one guy. It was only ever Tomic on his own." I held up one finger. "One man. One set of partials, one match of DNA, one any-fuck-ing-thing."

Before I could get angry with myself for being so blind to what now seemed so obvious, my phone rang in my hand. I was directed through HQ switchboard to speak to an official with access to consulate records. And in one phone call, the final piece of the puzzle fit into place.

Pavao Tomic was born five minutes before his identical twin, Rajko. Pavao had come to the US six years ago, which we already knew. Two years ago, Rajko had come to the US to visit his brother for three months and went back to Croatia but hadn't been seen or heard from since. He'd just disappeared.

The consulate official told me they had records of Rajko re-entering Croatia but had no record of him being there since.

"Because he's still in America," I told him.

I was met with silence as the official tried to understand something that didn't make sense.

"Are there any other relatives?" I asked.

"There's a cousin, Boris, who immigrated to the US four years ago."

"It wasn't Rajko who went home," I said. "It was Boris." I could hear the rustling of paper and the clicking of a keyboard, but for right now, I had all I needed. "Please forward all information to Ross Berkman, Narcotics Division. Mark it urgent."

I hung up and walked back to Kira. He was looking at me like I was something fascinating to watch, so I kissed him with a grin, just as my phone rang. It was Mitch. "What the hell is so damn important?"

"It's Tomic," I started. "I know why it never made sense. I know why we couldn't find the second person, Mitch. Because we weren't looking for two of the same guy."

There was silence on the other end of the line.

"Tomic has a twin, Mitch," I said. "An identical twin. Rajko Tomic is in the country illegally. He's been here for two years. And the reason why we had no record of him is because technically, he's not here."

I could hear what sounded like a car door shut in the background, and his response was short. "I'll be at the office in ten."

NOT EVEN AN HOUR LATER, I was in the office with Mitch, Kurt, Tony, and Berkman, explaining the whole development when my phone rang.

I didn't recognize the number. "Hello?"

"Detective Elliott?"

"Yes. Speaking."

"Did you get my message?" The accent was European.

"What message?"

"Mm," the voice mused. "Check with reception."

"Tomic?" I asked into the phone, and all eyes in the room stared at me. I had no idea how he'd got this number or what message he was talking about. "We're on to you. We know about your brother."

The voice laughed. "I'm on to you too, Detective Elliott."

The line clicked dead, and I looked at the silent men watching me, waiting. "He sent us a message. He said to check with reception."

As quick as I said the words, Berkman was on the landline, speaking with reception on the ground floor.

"What else did he say?" Mitch asked.

"He said he was onto me too."

"What does that mean?" Tony fired back, looking at everyone.

I answered him honestly with a shake of my head. "I don't know."

Berkman put the phone down. "There's a box at reception. It's been X-rayed," he said. All mail was. "It looks like a jacket?" His tone was disbelieving.

"A jacket?" Kurt quipped. "What the hell kind of message is a jacket?"

"Is it a brown jacket?" Mitch asked quietly, and when his eyes landed on me, I understood. The only person we'd seen wearing a brown jacket was our snitch.

"Ferret," I told them.

Berkman was back on the phone, ordering patrols to scour the docks in search of Ferret. The package was cleared, and when it was sitting on our desk, with gloved hands, I pulled out the familiar brown jacket. It was riddled with bullet holes and stained red with blood. Too much blood.

There was no note. There was no need for one. We got the message loud and clear. Not long after that, a uniformed officer arrived to tell us they just pulled a bullet-riddled body out of the water near the docks, matching Ferret's description.

Berkman was all action, giving orders, taking charge. "We can expect him to request the release of his brother, but what he wants to wager for that is anyone's guess."

Berkman ordered Kurt and Tony to speak to Pavao Tomic in his cell, to see if there were any clues about Rajko —what he was capable of, what he might do to up the ante.

"What are we doing, boss?" Mitch asked.

"Nothing." Then he turned to me. "Under no circumstances are you to leave the building. Tomic's words 'I'm on to you too' are a direct threat." And my boss looked worried. Then he pointed his finger at me. "It's a personal message to you, Elliott. Somehow he has your cell number. For some reason he's singled you out. You're not to do anything or go any-fucking-where."

"It's because the media flagged me as the leader," I bit back at him. "I'm the mouthpiece, so I'm the target. That's all." Realizing Berkman wasn't going to sway, I tried to reason. "We won't know what he wants until he contacts us again. It's not *me*."

Berkman's jaw bulged, and his temples swelled. "Elliott, don't argue with me," my boss barked at me. "You may as well get comfortable. Safest place for you is to be right here in this building."

Fuck. I snarled at Berkman, snatched my phone off my desk, and stomped over to the far end of the room. Taking a deep breath and trying to sound calm, I hit Kira's number. He answered with, "Hey, sexy."

I smiled, despite my mood. "Hey, baby."

"Let me guess," he said. "You'll be late tonight."

"Yeah, this Tomic case is about to go down." I took a deep breath. "Kira, he called me directly. Tomic called *me*."

There was silence for a moment and then a quiet, "He what?"

"He called my cell."

"Matt…"

"You said you wanted to know," I countered. "So I'm telling you."

He growled. "Fuck."

"Don't worry, babe," I said, trying to soothe him. "Berkman isn't letting me leave HQ. If Tomic wants me, he's gotta go through about a thousand cops to get me."

Kira's voice was quiet. "Do you think he'll try?"

"Honestly? No, I don't," I told him truthfully. "We won't know what his game plan is until we hear back from him. But Berkman isn't taking any chances."

Kira sighed. "Thank God one of you has the sense of self-preservation."

I huffed at him. "So you know I'm safe, okay?"

I could hear the smile in his voice. "Yeah, baby. Thank you."

I could also hear background noise. "Are you driving?"

He snorted. "Yes. Hands free, officer." I rolled my eyes, even though he couldn't see, but then he explained, "I'm closing up for Chris again tonight. I'm on my way there now."

I looked at my watch. Six o'clock. I didn't realize it had got so late. "I can't believe you'll be less than a block away, and I can't see you."

He laughed. "It's a shame. I kind of hoped you'd join me again tonight. There are no security cameras in the showers…" He trailed off suggestively.

I groaned, and he chuckled.

"Or I could fuck you on the mats, on a weight bench..."

I groaned louder, and he laughed.

"That's cruel," I told him. "I'll get you back for that."

"I sincerely hope so," he said with a laugh. "Okay, babe, I just pulled up. I gotta go. Call me anytime to let me know you're safe."

"I will," I promised.

"And Matt?"

"Yeah?"

"I love you."

I grinned. "You need your head read."

He laughed. "Wake me when you get in."

"I will." Smiling into the phone, I said, "And Kira?"

"Yeah?"

"I love you too."

<hr>

WHEN I WALKED BACK into the office, Kurt and Tony were back. They'd brought Chinese food with them, so we sat and ate while they relayed their meeting with Pavao Tomic.

"He didn't say a word," Kurt said, "until we mentioned the phone call and the jacket."

"What did he say then?" I asked with a mouthful of food.

"Nothing," Tony said. "But his eyes went wide, and he went real pale."

"Was he *scared*?" Mitch asked.

Kurt nodded, spearing another mouthful of food with his fork. "Shitless."

"He's scared of his twin brother?" I asked incredulously.

"Scared of what he's capable of," Tony told us. "We told him he's not responsible for anything his brother does, but if he knows something and doesn't tell us, he'll be charged as an accessory."

"What did he say to that?"

"He was silent for a long while," Kurt answered. "Looked all sorts of uncomfortable, then he said he didn't know anything, but even if he did, he wouldn't say." Kurt looked at me and said, "He said he'd rather do life in solitary confinement than rat on his brother."

Then Tony interjected. "But it was like he said that because he knew his brother would kill him if he talked."

"Did he say anything else?"

"Only that he's sorry for whatever his brother does," Kurt said, shaking his head. "He said we should take the threat very seriously."

Tony threw his empty Chinese container in the bin. "It doesn't matter much, because the sick sonofabitch is going down. He can spend forever in a cell with his brother."

Over the next hour or so, I pieced together the timeline from the information the Croatian authorities sent through and tried to concentrate on the files in front of me, but my mind kept wandering to Kira.

"You've got that 'I'm so in love' look on your face again." Mitch laughed.

I grinned at him, and looking around, I saw no one was paying much attention to us, so I asked, "Got a sec? Can we talk?"

"Sure," he answered.

I got up and led the way to the stairwell, suddenly very nervous about what I was about to tell him.

"What's with the secrecy?" he asked, then answered his

own question. "Oh, this is the big secret thing you've been trying to tell me for the last few weeks?"

I nodded and took a deep breath, struggling to know where to start.

"Jeez, Matt," he said. "You're really freaking out. You know Tomic can't get you in here."

I laughed nervously. "Ah, that's not it," I said. "It's about Kira."

"What about her?"

"That's just it, Mitch," I started to say. "Kira's not a her—"

Cutting me off, someone yelled out from inside our floor. "Elliott! Seaton!"

We jumped to our feet at the panicked tone. Mitch pulled back the door to find one of the guys on our floor looking for us. "Berkman wants you. Now! Now!"

His urgency set us in motion, and we raced to the boss's office at the opposite end of the floor.

"Where the hell were you?" he roared at us.

It wasn't him I looked at. It was Kurt and Tony. They were both pale white, and their eyes were wide. Something was very, very wrong.

It was then I noticed the TV screen.

"Ah, Detectives Elliott and Seaton," the now-familiar face said on the screen. Tomic. "So nice of you to join us."

All eyes were on the screen. It was a low-resolution recording, as though he was videoing this via a crappy internet connection, and the wanted man smiled, pure evil.

Berkman told us, "It's a live feed. He can see us and hear us, like we can see and hear him."

My heart was thumping, my adrenaline was spiked.

Tomic grinned. "You have something I want. I have something you want, something you all want."

The screen panned to the side, and my heart stopped. Literally stopped.

There on screen, huddled on the floor in some strange room, were Anna, Mitch's girlfriend; Evie, Tony's wife; and Rachel, Kurt's girlfriend.

They had tape over their mouths; their hands were bound together. Their faces were tear-streaked and frightened, and the room around me erupted.

All men were on their feet. There was noise and swearing and yelling, but I couldn't seem to hear over the blood pounding in my ears.

"Uh-uh." Tomic clicked his tongue, waving his finger at the screen. "I'm not done yet. I have one more surprise." Then he looked off screen and told someone to, "Bring in contestant number four."

And my stomach fell to my feet.

No. No, no, no. Please, dear God, no.

One of Tomic's men brought in someone with what looked like a pillowcase over their head. We couldn't see their face. But I knew who it was. I recognized the shirt. The gym shorts, his work uniform.

His hands were tied together behind his back. He was pushed to his knees, and I couldn't breathe.

Tomic ripped the cover off Kira's head. There was blood dripping from a cut over his eye. Tomic laughed. "See someone you recognize, Detective Elliott?" He grabbed Kira's face in his hand and shoved him toward the camera. "He's a fighter, this one. Took down three of my guys."

Someone beside me whispered, "Frankie?"

Tomic laughed again. "His name's not Frankie, is it, Detective Elliott?"

Everyone in the room turned to stare at me, but I couldn't seem to think. And my lungs wouldn't work right.

Tomic growled into the screen. "Tell them what his name is."

I had to force the air out of my lungs so I could speak. "His name is Kira."

Just like that, my life as I knew it was over.

CHAPTER FIFTEEN

NO ONE BLINKED. No one breathed.

Tomic's face closed in on the screen, and he smiled. "Have I got your attention, gentlemen?"

The screen went black.

Berkman was a flurry of action, barking orders, tracing internet connections, patrols to houses, other family members. Pavao Tomic was on lockdown and every available man was on the street. "We need to know where they're being held! Now, now, now!"

The entire building around us blurred into action.

The four of us didn't move.

I stared at the black screen, rendered incapable of moving, feeling, thinking...

Mitch spoke first. "He's got my Anna."

"And Evie."

"And Rachel."

I looked at them and swallowed. "And Kira."

I WASN'T sure how long after, a couple of minutes maybe, Berkman had other detectives asking us questions about the four hostages—their whereabouts, who they were with, who saw them last, possible witnesses. It shouldn't have been different when it was one of our own, but it was.

The detectives assigned to question us were good cops. We knew them. We outranked them. We were better at doing this than them. We were the best at what we did, yet there we sat, useless. Lost.

"When did you speak to Frankie last?" the detective asked.

"About six o'clock," I answered mechanically. "His name is Kira..."

Detective Cortez looked at me and nodded sympathetically. "Where was Kira tonight?"

"He was closing the gym for Chris." Like my mind was swimming through mud, I remembered..." There's surveillance at the gym. The main floor is covered with CCTV." I stood up, telling him, "We need to pull the surveillance!"

Cortez put his hand on my shoulder. "We'll get it." He darted out of the room.

Then I looked then at the other three. Mitch, Kurt, and Tony.

Tony sneered at me. "Frankie? *Frankie* is this Kira you're seeing?" His tone was biting, and his stare was pure disdain. "Never would have had you pegged as a fag."

My blood ran cold, and the room erupted around me. Everyone was on their feet, chairs and tables were pushed and shoved. I was trying to get my hands on Tony, but Mitch had me, pulling me in the opposite direction.

I could see Tony struggling in Kurt's grasp, and I hoped like all hell he got free so I could punch the crap out of him.

"Enough!" Berkman's voice boomed. "That's enough! You wanna kill each other?" he yelled, then pointed to the blank screen. "Then Tomic's already won. We stay together on this, because it's the only way we'll win." He stared at me, then at Tony. "Do I make myself clear?"

The four of us nodded, all breathing heavy. I glared at Tony. "Call me that one more time. I dare ya."

"Elliott!" Berkman reprimanded me. Then he turned to Tony. "One more derogatory comment outta you, Milic, and you'll be back on the beat. Understand?"

A tense silence settled over us, and the TV screen blinked on, earning our full attention. Tomic appeared on screen with a sinister smile. Even he could see the tension between us, the way we were on opposite sides of the room. "Didn't interrupt anything, did I?"

Tomic looked directly at me. "I take it your coworkers didn't appreciate being lied to, Detective Elliott. They had no idea who Kira was, did they? They didn't know it was a *man*, did they?" He shook his head. "It took a little bit of snooping. I must admit, I wondered who the girl was you were sneaking around with. It wasn't until your little weekend away together that I realized it wasn't a *girl* at all."

I could feel my blood boiling, and it wasn't until I felt Mitch grab my arm that I realized I was inching closer to the screen.

Tomic laughed. "You should tell your boyfriend not to make it so..." he trailed off, trying to find the right word, "... *unpleasant*... for himself."

He moved to the side then, allowing us to see behind him. The women were still huddled, clinging to each other and crying. Kira was now on the floor beside them. He was on his knees, kind of facing side on. I could see then, his feet were taped together. He had blood dripping from his nose, over the tape covering his mouth, and more blood coming from the gash over his eye.

Tomic clicked his tongue and sighed. "As you can see, we've had to restrain his feet. He's a feisty one."

"You leave him the fuck alone!" The words were out before I could stop them.

"Or you'll what?" Tomic leered at the screen.

Before I could answer, Berkman stood in front of me. "I am Ross Berkman, the officer in charge. What are your demands?"

Tomic looked at Berkman and grinned. "Thought you'd never ask." He tilted his head. "My brother, five million dollars, a plane to Dubrovnik with clearance to leave and land." He smiled like he'd just ordered lunch. "It's simple mathematics. Four things for me, four things for you." He looked back at the four hostages. "If I don't get one of my requests, you don't get one of yours."

My stomach twisted in knots.

"So, detectives," Tomic called out. "If you fail to deliver, their blood is on your hands." He smiled excitedly, and the screen went black.

Again the room flew into action. There were analysts, negotiators, psychologists, expert after expert, all talking, buzzing. I blinked in the white noise, trying not to think about what Kira had just gone through. I pulled at my hair and grabbed my stomach, ignoring the need to throw up.

"They're torturing him." My words were barely a whisper in a room full of noise, but Berkman heard me just fine. He nodded sadly. Bile rose in my throat, but Cortez burst into the room.

"We got footage!" he yelled. "No audio, but watch this!"

On another screen the footage started to play and we saw the familiar gym, people finishing up, talking. Kira walked onto the screen, smiling. He bumped fists with another guy. "That's Officer Sanchez," Cortez explained. "He was the last one there. He left at eight forty-seven."

We watched Kira on screen, setting up equipment, cleaning up, finishing off paperwork. Two minutes later, although he'd turned off some lights, we could still see the three men who ran into the room.

Kira spun around as the first guy struck at him. He blocked defensively, instinctively, and retaliated with swift hit-kick combinations.

The second attacker lunged at him, and Kira took him down with one swift kick to the head. The attacker hit the floor and didn't move.

"Jesus," someone behind me muttered. I didn't see who. "He's good."

The third attacker struck at him and was joined by the first attacker. It was now two against one. Kira held his own, this time taking out the third man with another hit-kick sequence.

But when the original attacker grabbed him, a fourth man walked on screen, hitting Kira in the ribs with a stun gun.

I watched as Kira's body arched and jerked before giving out, like some bad late-night movie in slow motion. The man behind him pushed him to the floor and proceeded to kick him in the ribs and stomach once, twice, three times.

Then he grabbed his arms, twisting them behind his back and taping them together. The third attacker stumbled over and punched him in the head twice, before they lifted him to his feet. The fourth man, who we could now see was Tomic, proceeded to hit him again with the stun gun.

My heart broke and bile rose in my throat.

The two thugs dragged Kira off screen, presumably out the front door. Tomic looked at the unconscious man on the floor, pulled out a pistol and shot him in the head. Right there, without a second thought.

The whole ordeal took less than two minutes.

Seeing it, watching it, knowing what they had done to Kira, burned in my stomach and lungs, and I felt like I was going to be sick.

"Homicide's got the gym covered," Cortez said quietly. "The place was wide open, body still on the floor."

Berkman looked at me. "I'm sorry you had to watch that."

The room spun, and there didn't seem to be enough air.

Berkman looked at me, concerned. "You okay?"

I nodded, unable to stop seeing in my head how they had hit him, kicked him, hurt him. I shook my head. "I think I'm gonna be sick," I admitted out loud.

Mitch picked me up by the tops of my shoulders like I was six years old and led me to the bathroom. I walked, somehow, and as soon as I was in the men's room, I couldn't hold it in. The horror, anger and fear bubbled in my stomach, and I threw up.

When I couldn't be sick anymore, I washed my face and rinsed out my mouth and stared at the unrecognizable man in the mirror. He was pale, scared. The man he loved had been kidnapped and beaten, he'd just been kicked out of the closet and one of his partners had called him a fag. I stared at my reflection. "How did it come to this?"

"Matt?" Mitch's voice startled me.

I jumped, turning around to see him behind me. I hadn't realized he'd stayed. He looked as scared and helpless as I felt. "Mitch?" I croaked. "I'm sorry."

He shook his head, and without making eye contact, he

said, "Not now. We need to get back." He turned and walked out on me.

I walked robotically back to the office. Berkman was busy with some guy in a suit, and amid the noise and commotion, the four of us sat in silence.

The next time Tomic appeared on screen, he was ranting about his brother, how he was the brains of the operation but too soft, how they were chalk and cheese, yet so very alike. His accent was thicker when he rambled, and my mind had trouble keeping up. He ranted about their childhoods, how they grew up, how when they were boys if one was naughty, they'd both be punished. Rajko told us how Pavao, sweet, quiet little Pavao, never did anything wrong, but he'd happily take punishments for his brother.

He didn't mention the hostages, though we could see them behind him, still sitting together on the floor. I couldn't see any noticeable changes in Kira's injuries, and I hoped he'd gone these last ten minutes without being beaten. I spent the entire transmission looking at his face, trying to see if they'd hit him again. His cheek looked a little bruised, though if it was a result from a previous beating or a new injury, I just couldn't tell.

When it seemed Tomic was winding down his little speech, Berkman asked if we could speak to one of the hostages. Tomic replied with a simple and cold, "No," and the connection was cut off again.

Kurt pushed a chair with his foot, sending it crashing into a desk. "We're meeting his demands, aren't we?" he asked, looking at Berkman. "Please tell me the whole 'we don't negotiate with criminals' doesn't apply here."

Berkman's face twitched. His lack of answer was an answer itself.

"Oh, you are kidding me!" Tony cried. "Give him whatever the hell he wants."

"You know we can't do that," Berkman said quietly.

"What the hell are we supposed to do?" Mitch snapped.

"I know what we're supposed to do," I told them. All eyes turned to me. "We find him first."

"Matt," Berkman warned. "You're all too close to this."

"We're the ones who should be in there!" I told him, speaking a little louder than I'd intended to. "We're the best chance we've got at getting them out alive. Let us do what we do best." I could see Berkman was considering it, so I added, "We're sitting here doing *fucking* nothing. We *know* this man. He's all we've studied for weeks."

Berkman looked at me, then at the other three men, and after a long moment, he sighed and nodded.

I stood up. "Right. I want a map of the city, some whiteboards. I want to speak to the brother. I want my files on Tomic—"

Mitch, Kurt, and Tony all looked at me, so I stopped talking and took a breath. Then quietly, I told them, "You can hate me for being gay tomorrow, but right now, we've got a job to do." The three of them stared at me. Maybe my comment about being gay shocked them. I didn't care. Right then, there were more important things. I pointed to the blank screen. "You can either watch me or help me, but either way I'm gonna find this sonofabitch, and then I'm gonna skin him alive."

I looked at their faces, and when my eyes met Mitch's, he smiled.

WE SET EVERYTHING up on the same wall as the video

linkup so when Tomic saw the room on screen, he couldn't see any of what we were doing.

Kurt calculated that the calls were coming at ten-minute intervals. "One forty-seven. One fifty-four. One fifty-two," he said out loud. "He's keeping all calls under two minutes."

"What does that mean?" Tony asked, rhetorically. "Is that some tracking buffer?"

Kurt frowned and admitted quietly, "I'm not sure."

Tony drew a radius of the target area of the city, using the gym as the center. Given it was the last point of contact at nine o'clock and the first video contact was barely half an hour later, taking into account traffic flow, Tony could calculate the maximum distances Tomic could have traveled in that time.

Mitch was working on the video footage with traffic control CCTV, trying to follow any possible suspect vehicles leaving the vicinity of the gym just before nine. I worked on replayed footage of the hostage scene, studying the room they were in, looking for clues, hints, anything. I purposely didn't look at Kira. I knew he was there, but I needed to focus. I needed to focus on anything but his cut face, his swollen eye, his rapid breathing, or what he'd been through. What he was going through.

So instead, I zoomed the footage in on the walls, the windows. It was a warehouse of some sort. Nondescript, no visible markers, and the windows were blackened by the night outside. By the time Tomic's face blinked onto the screen, I was none the wiser about where they were.

Tomic addressed Berkman, demanding to know if his deal was being met. He wanted to see his brother. Berkman countered this demand with his own. "Show us the hostages."

When Tomic moved from in front of the screen, we could see the four of them sitting on the floor. The women had been crying. Kira was still on his knees, but he was leaning a little to one side. He was breathing hard, and his face was etched in pain.

"What did you do you do to him?" I yelled at the screen.

Tomic spun to look at the screen, to look at me. "Your boyfriend really should mind his own business." Tomic looked back at Kira, then back to me. "He's so gallant. It really is admirable."

Then Tomic called out off screen, and one of his thugs, the guy from the docks, the one with the tattooed neck, appeared. He slunk down next to the three women on the floor and slowly reached his hand out, grabbing Evie, Tony's wife, by the arm.

Tony was suddenly beside me, and we stood, shoulder to shoulder, in front of the screen.

Evie cried out, and Kira leaped from his knees to his feet. He lunged at the man, but with his hands behind his back and his feet taped together, he didn't stand a chance.

The thug punched Kira hard in the stomach, connecting with a dull thump. We could hear the air leave Kira's lungs as he slumped back to his knees. It was like watching a nightmare play out in slow motion right in front of me.

The women shrieked, and Tomic's face appeared on screen, covering most of our view. "See? He just won't stay down. He won't let my men touch the women."

"Untie his hands and feet, you sonofabitch!" I yelled at the screen. "Make it a fair fight!"

Tomic smiled. "I am many things, Detective Elliott," he said. "Stupid is *not* one of them." Then his smile died abruptly, and he looked at Berkman. "My brother. Ten minutes."

Once again, the screen went black.

Berkman was back on his phone, trying to get Pavao Tomic cleared to be brought up to our office, while I stared at the screen. My heart was hammering, pounding against my ribs. All I could think about, all I could see in my mind, was how they had hit him, how they were torturing him. Acid burned in my stomach, and if I hadn't already been sick, I would have been again.

I felt a hand on my arm, and looked up. I expected to see Mitch or Berkman, but it wasn't. It was Tony.

He was scared. I could see it clear on his face, in his eyes, and he was sorry for calling me a fag. He was thankful for Kira. I could see it. He saw what I saw, how Kira was willing to try to save his wife from God only knows what. "He's protecting them," he said. Then he squeezed my arm and gave me a nod. "We'll find them."

Before I could answer, there was a knock at the door, and a woman walked in. "Detective Elliott," she addressed me. "Can I ask you something?"

She was one of the experts who'd been in and out a dozen times. I stared at her, waiting for her to continue.

"Ah..." She hesitated, looking around at the men in the room, "It's about Kira."

I blinked. "What about him?"

She turned to the computer tech guy who'd been helping me with the analysis of the videos. "Can you bring the footage up on screen?" When the familiar hostage scene appeared, she asked him to zoom in on Kira.

She looked at me and said, "At first I thought he was struggling with the feeling or the circulation in his hands, being they're tied behind his back..." She trailed off. "But now I'm not sure."

The screen was focused on Kira, and more specifically, his hands tied behind his back. Everyone in the room watched in silence. The woman, whose name I still didn't know, pointed to the screen. "See that?"

Oh, my God.

"Berkman!" I yelled, and my boss appeared in the door a second later. "I need an ASL translator. Now!" I turned to the video tech. "I want all footage on Kira and his hands, from the very beginning."

"What is it?" Mitch asked me, suddenly beside me.

"He's signing," I told everyone in the room. "He's trying to tell us something using sign language."

CHAPTER SIXTEEN

JUST AS HE'D SAID, Tomic appeared on screen ten minutes later. He spoke to Berkman and, noticing our obvious absence, wanted to know where we were.

"They've gone to escort your brother here," our boss lied. We were really in the next room, watching footage of Kira. Although Tomic couldn't see us from the video feed, we could see him on screen and hear every word he said.

The sign language translator explained whatever Kira was trying to tell us wasn't clear. From his side-on position, we could only see one hand, and being bound behind his back, his hand movement for signing was severely restricted.

We watched and re-watched, trying to piece together the puzzle. The first thing we could make out was when Kira held out three fingers, then did what looked like the sign for talking. It was quick, and we weren't even sure if we were seeing the whole message or just a part of it, or if he was using full words or if he was spelling.

Kurt held up his hands, gestured what looked like two birds squawking and groaned in frustration. "What does that mean?"

The translator shook her head. "With the hands held down low like they are, I'm not sure. But this," she said, mimicking the hand action and holding her hand up to her forehead, "means male."

Males. And three fingers. "Three males," I repeated. "There's three men."

The translator nodded and smiled. "I think so."

There wasn't much else to see, given that Tomic stood in the way or we couldn't see Kira's hands clearly or he was being hit. But the next time we could see him was after a particularly bad beating, his hands were shaking, but we could see what he was signing.

Kira formed his hand with his thumb, forefinger and pinky extended out and his middle and ring finger folded in.

"What does that mean?" Mitch asked.

The translator looked at me, but I was the one who answered. My voice was quiet, and I was sure they heard my heart break. "That's the sign for 'I love you.'"

Mitch's eyes softened, but before he could say anything, the translator called out, "Rewind that." She walked up close to the screen and pointed to where Kira curled his forefinger over, making a hook, but we lost visual when Tomic moved in front of him.

I stared at the translator. "What does that mean?"

She shook her head and shrugged in answer.

Fuck.

Tomic appeared on the live-feed, being fed bullshit by Berkman and two negotiators, while we watched from the next room. He was getting angrier and more frustrated that he'd not seen his brother, and when the telecast was cut a little short, Berkman scrubbed his hands over his face.

He walked out toward us, his expression grave. "He's running out of patience, and we're running out of time." He looked at the four of us. "We need to piece this together now. Tell me what we know."

"There's three men."

"They're within a fifteen mile radius of here."

"Tomic's keeping all telecasts under two minutes?"

"Why?" Berkman asked.

"We're not sure," Kurt said.

Berkman frowned. "What happens every two minutes that he doesn't want us to know?"

"Subway?" I offered.

"Airport?" Mitch said.

"Airport..." the translator repeated. "Airport! Of course! This"—she held up her hands in the 'I love you' sign —"means I love you when the hand is facing forward. But this," she said, pushing her hand facing down, outward from her chest, "means airplane."

The hairs on my neck stood on end.

"And this," she said excitedly, pointing to the screen, paused on footage of Kira's hooked finger, "if he could use both hands and curl one finger over the other, it means coat hanger."

"Coat hanger?" Berkman repeated disbelievingly.

Oh, my God. "Not coat hanger," I told them. "*Plane hangar.*"

"They're in a plane hangar," Mitch said, racing over to the map of the city.

Berkman grinned at me. "Your boy's one smart cookie."

The translator urged the video tech to replay the second video we saw. "At the very end of the feed," she said. We watched as the footage rolled. She pointed to the screen. "There!"

It was like Kira was flinching his hand, not signing anything. The footage paused to show as brief as it was, and the angle wasn't great, but he was pointing his index finger and thumb, then in slow motion, we watched as his hand closed in a fist before Tomic cut the feed.

"LA," the translator cried. She spun to look at us. "It's fast and the angle is wrong, but I think that's an L and then an A."

"They're in a plane hangar in LA?"

"No," the translator shook her head. "He didn't finish. I'd bet money the next letter was an X."

"LAX." I put it together. "They're in a plane hangar at LAX."

THE ENTIRE FLOOR flew into action. The four of us were on our feet, checking our guns, getting ready.

"Detectives," the film tech called out from across the room. "Tomic's back on screen. Detective Elliott, he's asking for you."

Knowing that could never be good, I walked hesitantly back to the office with a new sense of dread.

Tomic was on screen all right. And so was Kira. There were two thugs holding him. Kira was on his knees in front of a small table with his hands stretched out in front of him, tied to the table. He had blood dripping freely from the cut above his eye, his jaw looked bruised, and he was covered in a sheen of sweat.

He looked scared. Worse than that, he looked resigned.

It took everything in me not to reach out and touch the screen.

"Detective Elliott," Tomic addressed me. "There comes a time we reach the point of no return, when you can't go back. Don't you agree?"

"What are you talking about?"

"Your boyfriend's been misbehaving," Tomic said with an eerie calm. "Trying to give hand signals when I wasn't looking, apparently. One of my men saw him."

Oh Jesus, no.

"I really was hoping we could get through this ordeal without violence." He shook his head and clucked his tongue. "But I really need to make sure your boyfriend doesn't do that again," Tomic said, and my blood ran cold.

One thug pulled Kira's head back by his hair, and Tomic grabbed his face. "Can't talk with your hands if I break your arms, can you?"

Like the world disappeared, all I could see was Kira. I knew Berkman was yelling, pleading, but I couldn't hear what he was saying. I couldn't hear anything.

I couldn't see anything except how Kira's eyes closed as Tomic lifted a metal rod over his head, swinging it down onto Kira's outstretched forearms.

I heard the sickening noise—a wet snap and a muffled scream.

I could feel hands on me, grabbing, holding me back from Tomic's smiling face on the screen. "If I don't see my brother in ten minutes, I'll start breaking other parts."

"You'll be dead in ten minutes!" I screamed at him, but the screen just went black.

My world went dark. I didn't remember shoving a table across the floor or throwing a chair at the wall. But when Mitch grabbed me, holding me back, I saw the room around me was trashed and men were staring at me, with fear and pity in their eyes.

I could feel Mitch's hands on me as the weight of what just happened settled over me. The same hands that held me back were now holding me up.

I looked at Mitch and tried to tell him, but it only came out as a whisper. "I want to kill him."

He looked at me, and his eyes were fierce. He nodded. "Let's go."

"Boys," Berkman said flatly. He looked at the four of us. His sympathetic eyes settled on me. "SWAT's been briefed. You boys can't go in there."

Our response was immediate and in complete unison. There was no way we were not going. There was no way we could not be there when this went down. The four of us faced him down.

Berkman put his hands up, palms forward. "Right," he sighed. "But we don't go in. We wait and watch until the site is cleared and the hostages are safe. Understood?"

THE VAN RIDE to LAX was the longest five minutes of my life. The five of us—Berkman refused to let us go alone—sat with wide eyes and in complete silence.

The airport was business as usual, but we snuck through the commercial gates normally used by transport, trucks, and tankers. The airport officials reported dim lights in the old hangars now used for storage but had no record of registered users. Intel confirmed the suspicious activity, so we knew exactly where we were headed.

The van pulled up a few warehouses over, and we waited. Lining one wall of the van was a row of surveillance screens, and we watched as the heavily cloaked, heavily armed tactical response team got ready to move in.

No one made eye contact. No one made a sound.

It was as though we were watching something else. It was surreal. Horrific. As if all the years of training we'd had, training to be detached and calculating, meant nothing. And we sat with our hearts in our mouths as we watched the SWAT boys move in. Like black smoke, they crept around the building, surrounding each point of entry, and when we were given our signal, we slipped out of the van.

We ran quietly to the side of the hangar, and as hard as it was, knowing they were just yards away, we waited. When we were in position, hidden in the shadows, the SWAT team moved in.

We'd done this a hundred times. It was standard procedure, protocol.

I'd never been so scared in my entire life. It had only been seconds, barely enough time to think. My heartbeat measured each moment, hammering triple time.

A shrill scream cut the darkened night, and the men beside me jumped. It was a woman's scream, and I instinctively grabbed Mitch's arm. When gunshots rang out, all four of us panicked and started to move.

Berkman put up his hand. "Not yet."

Two more shots were fired, and I thought my heart would burst. Fear made it impossible to breathe.

After what felt like an eternity, Berkman's radio crackled loud in the silence. We had the all clear to move.

My body shot forward without conscious decision to do so. Kurt pulled the door open, and without knowing what would meet us, we raced inside.

Adjusting to the light, I scanned the large room, and when my eyes trained in on Kira, I ran. I didn't care that there were other cops or the SWAT team guys. I didn't even think.

Kira was sitting on the floor, his bound feet out in front of him, his arms against his chest, and I almost tackled him. I wrapped my arms around him and pulled him against me, mindful of his left arm. It was obviously broken—there was a lined dent above his wrist, and it was going purple. He slumped against me with relief and exhaustion.

I held him. I just held him, feeling him in my arms, his familiar body, the warmth of his skin. I kissed the side of his neck, the side of his head, all the while telling him he was okay. He was okay. I had him. He was safe.

Pulling his face into my hands, I looked him over, his bruised and bloodied, beautiful face. I slowly peeled the tape off his mouth, and he took sudden, deep breaths. I kissed his face, his hair, telling him it was all over.

I sat my ass on the floor and pulled him into my lap. I didn't want to let him go. I looked around then, at the other three guys, all in a similar position on the floor as me. They were doing the exact same thing—whispering, holding, rocking. I knew they saw me hold Kira and kiss him, and I knew they heard me tell him I loved him.

After years of hiding, of trying to keep my life a secret, I simply didn't care.

I now knew what really mattered. When the bullshit was stripped away, I could see with perfect vision what really mattered. So I held him a little tighter and kissed the side of his head again.

What happened after that was a bit of a blur. I remember seeing the bodies of the three men. I remember being disappointed that Tomic was dead. I'd wanted to kill him myself. I remember seeing Tomic's lifeless body and thinking this wasn't anywhere near as satisfying as it should have been.

I remember the scene around us, filled with uniforms and noise. I remember how the four of us cops sat huddled, cradling our lovers, while people worked around us.

I remember riding in the back of the ambulance with

the paramedics and arriving at the hospital, but it was all in slow motion and soundless, and I remember feeling heavy and numb.

I didn't remember conversations. I didn't remember ever speaking. As I looked around the waiting room at Mitch, Kurt, and Tony, I didn't remember walking in there. I remember the nurses and then doctors talking to me, but I couldn't remember what they said.

I did remember being told I had to wait. That was what I was doing. Sitting in the waiting room and... waiting.

I looked around at the three men waiting with me. None of us were the same men we were just a few hours before. We were forever changed.

It was after one o'clock in the morning. My head fell back against the wall behind me, and just for a moment, I closed my eyes.

I was startled when Berkman sat down beside me with a huff. "The media's all over this," he said with disdain. "It's a fucking circus."

So that was it. Just like that, it was done. I sighed. "My career is over." My voice sounded flat, even to me.

Mitch blinked tiredly and looked hard at me, obviously not up for riddles. "What do you mean?"

I shook my head. "Never mind," I said quietly, dismissively.

"You mean because of the gay thing?" Kurt asked bluntly.

I raised my eyebrows at him. "Gay thing?"

Berkman looked between the four of us, then at me. "They didn't know?"

Tony answered. "No, we didn't know."

I looked at Berkman. The way he asked the question was odd. "You knew?"

"Yeah," he shrugged. "It's not rocket science. You said Kira was Japanese."

I nodded.

"Well, Kira in Japanese is a guy's name," he said simply.

Oh. Of course. I shrugged. "I didn't think anyone would know..."

Mitch looked at me. His voice was quiet. "Why didn't you tell me?" Kurt, Tony, and Berkman stayed silent, knowing this was an issue between partners. "You should have told me."

"I tried," I told him honestly.

"The last few weeks? Is that what you've been trying to tell me?" he asked incredulously. I nodded, and he laughed without humor. "What about the last two years, Matt? We've been *partners* for two years." He swallowed loudly. "You *lied* to me."

"I never lied," I said defiantly, getting to my feet. "I never said *she* or *her*. You guys did, not me."

"But you never corrected us either!" Mitch cried. "Have I ever given you reason to think I wouldn't accept it?"

I shook my head and conceded, "No."

When I looked at him, I could see his issue wasn't with me being gay. It was honesty. The fact I'd kept the truth from him was what hurt him the most. He looked like he'd been through hell. He had. We all had.

"Then why?" he growled at me.

"Because I'm a *good* cop," I told him. "I'm a great cop, a tough cop, a fair cop." He looked at me, confused. So I spelled it out for him. "As soon as the media finds out," I said, pointing toward the outside window, "no matter what the hell I do after today, no matter how many drug-rings I bust, no matter how many lives I save, I'm nothing but a *gay* cop."

"Is that what you meant when you said your career's over?"

Before I could answer, two doctors walked into the room. The other four men joined me standing. "How are they?"

The first doctor said, "Gentlemen," in greeting. He seemed to hesitate, then he cleared his throat. "We just need to clarify which of you are related to the victims. Mr. Milic, your wife is Evie, yes?" They weren't supposed to divulge patient information to non-relatives.

Tony nodded, "Yeah, but we're all family here."

The doctor hesitated again, and Berkman's jaw bulged. "I'm Ross Berkman," he said in his usual gruff tone, making the two doctors look at him. "I'm the Commanding Officer, Narcotics Division of the LAPD, and request full disclosure under the Law Enforcement Access to Patient Information Act."

The first doctor looked at Ross, and then at the four of us. He didn't even ask what it was we wanted to know, he just told us, "The three women are shaken and in shock, considering what they've been through, but physically they're unharmed. We'll give them something to help them sleep, but they can go home in about half an hour."

Everyone in the room breathed.

The second doctor said, "All reports say the same thing. If it weren't for Mr. Franco, it could have been a very different story. According to all three women, Mr. Franco put himself between them and the attackers."

I was almost scared to ask. I took a step closer, and my voice croaked. "Is he okay?"

The first doctor looked at me apologetically, as though he was unsure if he should answer. Ross put his hand on my shoulder and waited until the doctor spoke. "He's taken one hell of a beating. His left arm was badly broken and needed surgery. He has two plates in his arm. He has three broken ribs, stitches above his eye, and a lot of abrasions. We've run X-rays and scans. There's no fractured skull or internal injuries—"

I sucked back a ragged breath. "Can I see him?"

The doctor hesitated, but Berkman glared at him. The doctor rolled his eyes, and I was led down a hall. When the doctor stopped at a door, he looked at me and spoke softly. "We've given him something to help him sleep."

I was frozen, unable to move. Fear rooted my feet to the floor. A hand touched my shoulder, and Mitch's voice behind me told me it was okay.

I could see Kira on the bed, lying still and quiet. My eyes stung, and I willed myself not to cry. He was so broken, so vulnerable.

Like I was made of lead, I somehow walked past machines to the far side of the bed. He'd been cleaned up. The dried blood was gone, replaced with bandages and bruises. I was scared to touch him.

I leaned down and kissed his lips, his bruised and swollen lips. I knew he was sleeping and couldn't hear me, but I told him anyway that I was sorry and I loved him.

When I looked up, Mitch was still there watching me. I was so tired and scared and relieved and sorry. I tried not to cry.

Then Kira's mother, Yumi, was there, rushing into the room. I was too tired to be surprised to see her. She touched my arm, but didn't look at me—her concern was for her son. Sal stepped around Mitch, and the tall, silent man, Kira's father, stared at me.

What could I say? What could I possibly say for what I had done to his boy? I lifted my right fist to my heart, drawing circles over my chest. I did it again and again, telling him over and over I was sorry.

I was so fucking sorry.

Mitch watched as Sal pulled me into his arms, and I couldn't hold back the tears. Kira's father held me as I fell to pieces in his arms and cried.

When I looked at Mitch, he was staring at me with sad, glistening eyes. He gave me a nod then turned and walked away.

Sal cupped his large hand on my cheek, making me look at him. His eyes flickered to Kira and then back to me. He led me over to the bed, and I quietly told them what I knew about his injuries, what he had gone through, how brave he had been.

"They took him from his work," I told them, wiping my face. I tried to talk clearly so Sal could read my lips. "It took four of them. He fought back so hard. Then they took him to an airplane hangar at LAX and they beat him." I couldn't stop the tears. "He tried to fight them. And he put himself between the attackers and the women to protect them. He was so brave, and they singled him out because of me and I'm so sorry."

Yumi started to cry, but she leaned up and wiped my face. "Matt, it's not your fault."

"Look at him," I cried, looking over the broken man in the bed. "Look at what I did to him!"

"You didn't do this," Yumi said. "That bad man they show on the TV did this."

"He did it because of me!" I said, wiping my cheeks with the back of my hand.

Sal put his big hand on my shoulder, and when I looked at him, he shook his head. Then he walked around to the other side of the bed and gently laid his hand on Kira's head. He stared at his sleeping form for a long while, then he looked up at me. He signed something, which Yumi translated. "Kira loves you. You need to let the guilt go. It not yours to own."

I took a deep breath, and a step away from the bed, giving them time with Kira. I didn't want to hear them pacify me and make excuses for me, but it certainly wasn't the time to argue.

Yumi looked back over her son and put her hand on his arm, and for a long while, they were quiet. Then she asked, "How long will he be in the hospital for?"

I wiped my face again. "I don't know. I think the doctor said they'll be back first thing in the morning."

Yumi wiped my face, gave me a hug, and smiled through her tears. She explained how the phone had rung, some channel wanting the scoop on Kira. "I hang up, and it rings again, but this time it was the hospital. How do the TV people know before the parents? The next of kin?" She was angry and scared, and I didn't blame her.

I looked at my watch. It was 3:35a.m. "Are there TV crews outside the hospital?"

Yumi nodded. "Everywhere."

A wave of exhaustion rolled over me. I think I swayed, because Sal put his hands on my shoulders to keep me steady.

"You should sleep," Yumi said softly.

I shook my head. "I'm not leaving."

She nodded, then had a sign-conversation with Sal that I didn't even pretend to follow. Then Yumi said, "We go now. We have seen him, and you with him, so we know he be okay. We will come back first thing when the doctor is here." She smiled kindly, motherly. "Is there something you need?"

I had no idea. I couldn't think, so I just shook my head. Instead, I told them I loved their son. I *loved* him, and I hoped to God he could forgive me.

Kira's mom looked at me sadly. "You so tired, Matt," she said. "He's sleeping. You should do the same."

I didn't wait for them to leave before I sat on the edge of the bed, and taking up as little room as possible, I lay down on my side next to Kira. Resting my head on the inside of my arm, I looked at the side of his face and listened to his soft breathing, until my eyes wouldn't stay open any longer.

Sometime later, a nurse came in with a blanket, telling me I couldn't sleep on the bed. She pulled out the chair, helped me into it and threw the blanket over me.

THE NEXT THING I KNEW, it was daylight. My body ached, and I heard voices and footsteps.

Then I remembered where I was.

I sat bolt upright, trying to get my bearings, when I saw him.

Kira was awake, and there was a nurse talking to him, but I went to him and took his right hand like she wasn't even there. His left eye was almost swollen shut, the bruises were highly colored and swollen, and he had small cuts everywhere.

"Hey," I breathed.

He squeezed my hand, and his voice was soft and croaky. "Hey."

Leaning in, I kissed his swollen lips softly. If he was surprised at my public display of affection, I couldn't tell. "I don't care who sees," I told him. His one good eye blinked slowly, then looked at me for a long moment. Maybe it wasn't the right time, but I said it anyway. "I was so scared, baby." I swallowed my emotions. "I was so scared."

He nodded. His good eye closed, but his hold on my hand tightened.

He was quiet, and considering what he'd been through, it was to be expected. He picked at his breakfast and answered all questions with a small nod or a slight shake of his head.

His room was constantly busy. His mom and dad were there before seven, bringing a change of clothes for both of us and some coffee for me. "You okay?" Yumi asked.

I shrugged. "Thank you for the clothes and the coffee."

She scowled at me for not answering her, but her attention was quickly drawn to Kira. They fussed over him and all I could do was watch and try to smile.

The doctor came in and looked Kira over, asked him some questions, and wrote things down in his file. Then before he left, he looked at Kira and said, "Any questions?"

Kira didn't hesitate. His voice was quiet but clear. "Can I go home? Please. I don't want to be here."

My heart clenched in my chest, but the doctor just smiled. "I'll see what I can do."

Before lunch, a nurse came in, taking observations, telling us the doctor said if Kira promised complete bed rest, he might even be allowed to go home today. Needless to say, Kira said he'd do whatever it took.

But the most surprising visitor was Berkman.

He poked his head around the door, saw me, and smiled. He looked... older. Like last night had aged him ten years. "Just checking in on our hero," he said as he walked in.

I smiled at my boss and introduced him to Kira's parents. When Sal signed hello, Berkman looked to me and smiled with an understanding nod. "Ah, that explains the sign language!"

I smiled, and taking a deep breath, I introduced him to Kira.

"Ross Berkman, my boss, I'd like you to meet Kira Takeo Franco." Then I added, "My boyfriend."

Berkman didn't bat an eyelid. "It's an honor to meet you, Kira," he said, shaking his hand. "You saved my entire team last night."

Kira blinked and answered softly. "I, um, no, I just—"

Berkman interrupted him. "Don't argue with me, son." I chuckled, knowing Berkman and his no-nonsense, boss-of-police attitude. "I saw the whole damn thing," Berkman went on to tell him. "And you're front page news."

Kira looked at me, then back to Berkman, wincing at the sudden movement. His voice was quiet. "Is it bad?"

Berkman sighed and nodded. "Don't have anywhere you can hide out for a week or two while this blows over?"

I looked at Kira. "Actually, we do." Turning to Yumi and Sal, I asked them, "If it's all right with you, maybe I could take Kira to the cabin. He'll need complete rest, and it's so peaceful there. I can look after him there, without worrying about anyone finding us."

Yumi nodded and smiled. "Of course. Good idea."

Kira tried to sit up, but wincing and holding his side, he settled back on the bed. I was quick to reach out, not sure where to touch him. "Are you okay?"

He breathed out slowly and gave me a nod. "How do we leave here?" He looked at me and mumbled. "If they know..."

Yumi snorted. "I'll send your father out to listen to all they have to say. He can sign them a press conference. It will keep them all busy for a while."

Sal rolled his eyes, and I couldn't help but chuckle. Berkman grinned, and even the corner of Kira's swollen lip curled upward.

I took his hand and told him, "We walk out of here with our heads held high. I'm not hiding anything from anyone anymore."

CHAPTER SEVENTEEN

IT WAS Berkman who called an impromptu media conference out in the front of the hospital, which allowed us to leave undetected. Kira said he wasn't up for the press, and I didn't argue. The paparazzi, looking for the photo of LAPD's golden boy with his *boyfriend*, thankfully hadn't tracked us down. The cabin was peaceful, remote, and private. It was perfect.

Kira was quiet and reserved for the first three days after he left the hospital. He dozed on and off most of the time, though it was a fitful sleep at best. He tossed and turned, and woke up panting and sweating.

For a man who last week would eat like a horse and wouldn't take even a Tylenol, he didn't eat much at all and took his pain meds without so much as a second look. His movements were slow and pained, and he liked me near him all the time.

The doctors told us that bouts of depression, anger, and frustration would be frequent, and not to take it personally. He was scheduled to speak to an LAPD counselor trained in how to deal with the aftermath of what he'd been through. All four of them—Kira, Anna, Evie, and Rachel—were scheduled at Berkman's insistence. Kira said he'd go, but he hadn't mentioned it since.

We spent most of our days on a lounge chair on the veranda, surrounded by trees, overlooking the mountains. He'd lie between my legs with his back to my front, his head on my chest, and even though it was peaceful, his silence was wearing me down.

I didn't want to push him, but the guilt of his ordeal was a weight I just couldn't carry. I told him I was sorry. I told him a hundred times. He dismissed me, telling me it was hardly my fault, but his ongoing silence told me otherwise. I tried not to make it about me, because it wasn't. It wasn't about me at all. It was about him.

But by the end of the first week, I almost had myself convinced he was going to leave me, and deep down, I knew he'd be better off without me.

"You okay?" His quiet voice brought me out of my musing.

Even a week later and his eye was healing nicely, though he'd have a scar through his eyebrow. His face was still a little swollen and bruised, but the colors were fading from deep purples to yellows and greens. The cuts were healing, his ribs were still sore, and his left arm ached and itched under the cast. Every one of his injuries hurt me. I smiled weakly. "Yeah, I'm okay."

His brow creased. He knew I was lying. "Will you tell me what's wrong?" he asked me quietly.

I couldn't. I didn't want to be the one who brought it up. His impending goodbye would kill me. So instead I answered him with a question, changing the topic completely. "Did you want to go for a walk? You haven't been for a walk in a week, let alone a run."

He shook his head no. "If you want to go back to the city, we can," he said out of the blue.

"What?" His statement surprised me. "I don't want to go back."

"Then why won't you look at me?"

My face fell, and after a long moment, my voice was just a whisper. "I don't want you to tell me goodbye."

After another moment of silence, I looked at him. He looked... confused. "What? Why would you say that?"

"I don't blame you for blaming me," I told him. "I mean, if it weren't for me and my job, none of this—"

His fingers to my lips stopped my words. "I don't blame you," he said with quiet determination. "*You* blame you."

"You *should* blame me."

"Stop telling me what to feel!" His anger surprised me.

"I'm sorry."

"And stop apologizing!" he yelled at me. Just like that, after a week of almost complete silence, the floodgates opened.

"I'm sick of hearing how fucking sorry you are," he yelled. "And you think I would *leave* you? After everything I went through?" He thumped his hand against his chest. "The only thing I could think about, while they fucking tortured me, was *you!*"

Tears welled in his eyes, but he blinked them back. "So don't you dare feel fucking guilty over what happened, Matt, because if I had to, I'd go through it all again."

He was so mad, and I didn't dare speak. I deserved his anger. I wanted him to be angry at me.

"I'd do it all over again," he repeated. "Because I love you."

He paced and when he turned back to face me, he was so mad. "So don't you dare tell me I'm better off without you. I went through that hell just to see you again." Kira pulled at his hair. "Even when they broke my arm, Matt, it didn't matter. None of it mattered. If they knew we were together or the whole damn world knew I was gay, it didn't fucking matter."

"How could it not matter?" I asked.

"Because being put through hell put my life into perspective, Matt," he cried. "If I didn't know what was important to me before, then I sure as hell do now."

When he turned too quickly, he winced and staggered at the pain in his ribs, and tears sprang to his eyes and a pained sob escaped him.

I rushed to him. "Kira..."

"I was so scared," he said, as the first of his tears fell. "I was so scared."

I pulled him against me as gently as I could and wrapped him up in my arms as he sobbed.

He sagged against me and finally let himself cry. The horror of what he'd been through, the emotions of this last week, all came tumbling out.

Through his tears and mine, he finally told me how he felt.

"I was so scared," he said. "For the women, for me, for you. I didn't know if they had you too. If you were even alive..." He cried harder. "I didn't know if they were going to kill me, but I couldn't let those bastards touch those women, Matt. I'd rather die protecting them than live with myself if I'd just done nothing."

Then he said, "I didn't even know if you would see me trying to sign behind his back." He shook his head. "I knew the words wouldn't make sense, but if anyone could make sense of it, I knew you would. I didn't know if you even saw any of it, but I had to do something."

"You did real good, baby," I told him, wiping his face and holding him tighter. "It was how we found you. It's because of you we knew where you were. You saved them, Kira."

"I couldn't bear the thought of never seeing you again," he admitted, wiping away his tears. Then he pulled back and looked at me with pleading in his eyes. "So please don't tell me I'm better off without you, because it would mean I went through all that hell for nothing. Don't tell me you're not worth it, because you are the only thing that is worth it, Matt."

I nodded and kissed him, wiping the salt water from his cheeks. "I won't. I promise," I vowed. "I'll never push you away."

He took a deep breath and exhaled shakily. "As if it weren't bad enough then," he said. "Now I feel like this. Like I'm... ugh." He groaned.

I held his face and made him look at me. "Like what?"

He shrugged and his whole body shuddered. "Like I'm in someone else's skin." He squirmed. "It's hard to explain, but it's like mine doesn't fit me anymore."

"Oh, baby."

"Will you help me?"

"Anything," I breathed. "I'll do anything for you."

"Make me yours," he said. His eyes were wide and full of fear. "Show me who I am, who I belong to."

I blinked, not sure what he meant.

He kissed me, hard and sure. His tongue invaded my mouth forcefully, abruptly. I pulled his face from mine. "Kira..."

"Take me to bed," he pleaded. "Take me. Top me. I need to feel... something. I need you."

There was desperation in his voice, in his eyes, and when he kissed me again, I could taste it on his tongue. I'd only topped a few times before—and never with Kira—I'd always felt the need to be taken care of. But this was different.

This wasn't my need. It was his.

I cupped his face, bringing my nose to his. His dark eyes were boring into me, begging. I kissed him softly, took his hand, and led him upstairs. Mindful of his injuries, I took my time getting him ready. He was glorious. His body, his smell, the feel of him in my hands, in my mouth as I sucked and licked him, while pushing my fingers inside him.

When he was naked on the bed before me, I readied myself with a condom and more lube, knelt between his thighs and gently lifted his legs.

I didn't push his legs too high, careful not to put weight on his ribs. "Tell me to stop if it hurts."

He nodded, and when he sucked back a breath, I pushed into him.

He closed his eyes, and his breathing hitched as I sank deeper inside. And when his eyes opened, silent tears ran down to his temples.

I froze. "Kira?"

He nodded. "Don't stop." Then he groaned. "Please, don't stop."

Leaning on one elbow to keep the weight off his ribs, I slowly started to thrust.

I didn't think about how tight it was, how hot he felt around me. I didn't think about how good it felt.

I thought about him.

I kissed him softly and told him I loved him. I traced my

fingers over his still-blackened eye and told him he meant everything to me. I shuddered, trying to stave off my orgasm, and I whispered in his ear how he belonged with me, how he belonged *to* me.

Thrusting as slowly as I could, I kissed down his neck, making him moan, and I knew I wouldn't last much longer. With my free hand, I took his cock between us and pumped him. I thrust my tongue into his mouth, while I thrust my cock into his ass.

And when he cried out, I thought I'd hurt him, but then his ass clenched around me and his cock erupted in my hand. Watching as pleasure rolled through him, being inside his body when it happened, pushed me over the edge. I could feel myself swell and surge while still inside him, and I came.

When I floated back into my body, we were on our sides, facing each other, wrapped in each other's arms. I could feel the fingers of his casted arm in my hair, and when I opened my eyes, his face was barely an inch from mine.

He looked serene.

"Thank you," he murmured and pecked my lips with his. He stared at me for the longest time, but eventually, he said, "We should get cleaned up."

"I'll do it," I murmured. "I'll take care of you," I told him, the same way he took care of me. "I just need to wait for the bones not to be jelly in my body."

Then I heard the most beautiful sound, a sound I hadn't heard in what felt like forever—the sound of Kira laughing. I smiled at him, taking in his still-bruised, still-beautiful face. I told him I loved him before I cleaned us up, and when I crawled back into bed and pulled him into my arms, I told him I loved him again.

He sighed contentedly, and the even rise and fall of his chest against mine lulled me to sleep.

———

I WOKE up to the familiar feeling of being watched.

When I opened my eyes, it was barely morning, and Kira was looking at me. He was on his side, resting his head on his not-broken arm, tracing the fingers on his casted arm up my chest. He smiled. "I'm starving."

I blinked myself awake. It was the first time he'd had an appetite in a week.

"I thought we could walk down to the coffee shop," he said, still smiling. "And maybe grab some breakfast."

I grinned at him. "Sure, babe. Just let me get dressed."

When I came out of the bathroom, he was holding my phone. "It beeped," he explained. Then looking at me, he said, "You've got a lot of missed calls."

"I've had it on silent all week." I shrugged. "They can wait."

He frowned but said nothing. He put on his Lakers cap, and we took it easy on the walk into town. We'd been so cut off from the rest of the world for the last week, I had no idea what the media had said about their "golden boy" or the whole Tomic ordeal, for that matter. If the girl behind the counter in the café recognized us, she didn't let on.

We ordered breakfast, and while we waited, Kira asked me if I'd spoken to Mitch.

I shook my head. "No."

"You need to talk to him."

"I know," I said with a nod, turning my cell phone over in my hands.

"He's your partner," Kira reminded me. Then he added softly, "I'd like to know how Anna is."

Shit. I'd been so caught up in my own misery, I didn't even realize... I reached over the table between us and squeezed his hand with one of mine, and pressed redial on my phone with the other.

"Mitch?" I knew my name came up on his screen, but I told him anyway. "It's me."

CHAPTER EIGHTEEN

THE CAR PULLED in front of the cabin, and Mitch got out first. He quickly went to the passenger side door and helped Anna out.

Physically, she looked fine. She looked tired, but no cuts or bruises. Not that I could see, anyway.

I walked out to meet them. Mitch gave me a smile and a bit of a hug, but turned and looked expectantly at Anna. I took her hand. "You okay?" I asked, quietly.

She gave me a sad smile. "I will be."

I nodded and gave her a proper hug. Only Anna pulled away, looking at me with tears in her eyes. "Where's Kira?"

"He's inside."

"How is he?"

"Tired and sore," I told her truthfully. "He's angry and frustrated, but he's strong."

Anna nodded. "And how are you?"

"I'm okay," I answered reflexively.

The front door opened then, and Kira limped outside. It was then that Anna saw his blackened and still swollen eye, his cut lip, the stitches in his eyebrow, his bruised jaw, and of course, his broken arm.

Anna gasped, and her hand went to her mouth and she started to cry. But she raced to him and threw her arms around him. "Oh my God," she sobbed.

Kira winced and hissed, the embrace obviously smarting his ribs, and Anna was quick to pull back. "Oh, I'm sorry," she said, unsure of where to touch him.

"It's okay," Kira answered. He put his hand on her arm. "Please tell me you're okay. And the others? Are they okay?"

"I'm okay," she said, and tears fell down her cheeks. "The others are all okay too. Thanks to you, we all are." Then Anna raised her hand to Kira's face. "But look at you. You're so hurt... what they did to you..." She wiped her face but only cried harder. "I see it over and over in my mind, Kira. What you went through. I'd hate to think what they would have done to us if it weren't for you."

Kira frowned, and I could tell he was fighting back tears. "I wouldn't have let anything happen to you."

Then Mitch stood beside Anna and extended his hand. "Thank you, Frankie. For what you did, for everything. I'll never be able to repay you."

Kira's eyes darted to mine. "Shall we go inside?" Kira shuffled back to the door. "Come in, I'll get us a drink."

When I'd first called Mitch, my first question was to ask him if we were okay. I had no idea if I still had a partner or even a friend. It wasn't an easy phone call. He was obviously hurt that I'd kept something important from him, and I couldn't blame him for that. Though he understood why I'd kept my sexuality hidden, it still stung that I'd hidden it from him.

He'd asked me how Frankie was, and I told him the truth. It was the first time I'd spoken to anyone about how he was doing, and it wasn't until I had to say it out loud that I realized how hard it was.

I hadn't been embarrassed that I'd cried to him on the phone. Mitch was the closest person I had to a brother. I didn't know if he was crying, but he'd breathed hard and his voice caught a lot as he talked about how Anna was doing.

I'd asked him to come up to the cabin. He asked Anna, and she was just as keen to see Kira as he was to see her. So he'd said they'd be up first thing.

Kira made coffee, and both Anna and Mitch watched him move slower and more calculating. "I'm sore today," he told them. "I think my body isn't used to being so caught up."

I walked into the kitchen and helped him with the cups and got the cream from the fridge. I looked at Kira. "You want me to help?"

"No, I'll do it," he answered. I didn't want him to think I was treating him like an invalid, so I didn't argue.

"You guys want breakfast?" I asked Mitch and Anna.

"We grabbed something on the way," Mitch said.

"Just as well," Kira said. "You don't want Matt to cook."

I smiled at the fact that Kira was making jokes. He was certainly coming out of the depression funk he'd been in. It'd only been a week, and to see him smile made me smile right back. I put my hand on the small of his back.

Mitch and Anna were both still watching us, and it occurred to me that this was the first time they'd seen Kira and me together. As a couple. Actually, it was the first time they'd seen me as part of a couple, with anyone, let alone a guy.

Anna smiled at us sweetly, and Mitch looked a little weirded out, but then he said, "Yeah, Matt's never been a good cook. Can't even work a grill."

Kira snorted. "Good to know some things never change."

Mitch smiled, and Kira handed him a mug of coffee. "Looks like you don't even let him make coffee."

"Not if I can help it," Kira said. "Well, not if I'm drinking it."

"Yeah, yeah," I said, taking a mug of coffee from Kira. "Pick on me, I don't mind. He rarely drinks coffee anyway. He prefers that healthy, yogurt shit."

Anna took her cup and looked around the cabin. "So, is this place yours?"

"It belongs to my parents," Kira said. "I spent a lot of time here as a kid."

"It's beautiful," Anna said.

Kira nodded. "We can go up and sit on the deck, if you want. It's lovely up there."

"Okay," Anna said.

We headed for the stairs, and I took Kira's coffee so he could climb up without worrying about balance and over-stretching very sore muscles. When I got to the top, knowing we had to walk through the bedroom, I was very grateful we'd half made the bed. The covers were up, not neatly, but at least it didn't look like we'd just had a romp in it.

Mitch had a lot to deal with getting used to having a gay partner, the last thing he needed to be reminded of was the said gay partner having sex. I wanted him to be cool with it. I didn't want to flaunt anything unnecessary in his face and ruin it all, if all he needed was some time.

I didn't want to lose my partner, but most of all, I didn't want to lose my friend.

We sat at the patio table on the deck. It was mid-morning, the sun was mild, the breeze was fresh and the birds were still singing. It really was peaceful.

"This is amazing," Anna said.

"It sure is," I replied.

"And you had us guys thinking you were camping out in the wilderness!" Mitch said, sipping his coffee. "This looks like five-star camping to me."

"Yeah, this is about as roughing it as I get," I answered.

Then it was quiet, no one really knowing what to say. I didn't want it to be like that. I didn't want uncomfortable silences with Mitch.

"Can we just talk about it?" I asked. "Can I just bring it up, so we can get it out of the way? I don't want there to be awkwardness between us, Mitch. I'm gay, always have been, always will be. And I need to know if you can forgive me for not telling you."

Kira reached his broken arm over and put his hand on my leg. I smiled at him, but then I looked back at Mitch. "I'm sorry I never told you, Mitch," I said truthfully. "I told myself for two years I wasn't lying to you. It was more that I wasn't divulging information. You never talked about what you did in your bedroom, and neither did I." I swallowed hard. "But I never lied to you, Mitch. I never said the word *she* or *her*..." I sighed. "But I never said *he* either."

"I get it," Mitch said, looking at me. "I do. I get why you didn't say anything. While I wish you felt you could have, I understand why you didn't. It can't have been easy."

I shook my head. "No, it wasn't."

"I don't blame you," Mitch said. "For what it's worth, I

don't blame you for not telling me, or making it public. I mean at first, I was pissed off because of the whole trust thing, but I get it now. Being a cop is hard enough, without having to defend yourself against your own as well." Then he looked straight at me. "I don't care about who's gay or not. Because at the end of the day, it's no one else's business."

"Thank you. For what it's worth, Mitch," I replied with a smile. "It means a lot to hear you say that."

Then Mitch put his coffee mug to his lips and smiled behind it. "Can I ask something? You know, if we're doing the whole honesty thing."

"Sure."

"Did you ever... you know... *like* anyone... that we might work with, or me, for that matter? Because I fill out a pair of jeans pretty well, you know."

"It's true," Anna said. "He does."

I barked out a laugh. "Um, no. Sorry to burst your bubble. But you're like my brother, and that's kind of gross."

Mitch laughed, relieved. "Just asking, you know, while we're clearing the air."

I shook my head at him, but thankful he was joking like always with me. Then I asked the dreaded question. "What about Tony and Kurt? Have you spoken to them? Are they okay with it?"

Mitch nodded. "They're okay, I think. Everyone's been lying low this week, keeping to ourselves, but I have spoken with them. They asked if I'd spoken to you, how you were, how Frankie was, that kind of thing. They were worried. You should call them."

"I haven't been able to face anyone this week," I admitted. I squeezed Kira's hand that was resting on my thigh. "I haven't seen any media reports, haven't watched TV. God, I haven't even spoken to Berkman, though he's left a bunch of messages on my cell. I just wanted to let it all settle down, I guess. And being here with Kira was my first priority. I don't care about what some checkbook journalist says about me."

"Berkman's been calling every day," Mitch said. "He's stopped by to see us a few times. He's worried about you. He knew you were going off the grid for a while, so he's been more patient than he's used to, but still..." Mitch sipped his coffee. "I think he was more worried that I hadn't spoken to you either. But I called him after I'd spoken to you yesterday, just so he'd stop worrying."

"I should call him," I admitted. "And Kurt and Tony."

"Yeah, you should," he said quietly.

Then Kira shifted in his seat and groaned a little. "Are you okay?" I asked him, putting my hand on his knee.

"Yeah, just getting sore," he said, twisting his torso, trying to stretch his back without hurting his ribs. "I actually think I need to go for a walk or something. I don't think my body is used to being so still for so long."

"I'll walk with you," Anna said. "It'll give us a chance to chat while these two talk about work."

"Okay," I said, trying not to sound too cautious. "We might walk down to the café later for lunch. So be careful not to overdo it."

Kira rolled his eyes at me, but he said, "We won't go too far."

Kira and Anna walked back inside, leaving Mitch and me alone. We still hadn't spoken by the time we watched Kira and Anna slowly walk, with arms linked, from the cabin into the woods.

Mitch spoke first. "How is he really?" he asked.

"Frankie, Kira, how is he really? He says he's okay, but he's not exactly moving real fast."

"You should see his torso," I said. "He's covered in bruises. His ribs..." I shook my head. "He has big angry black and blue blotches."

Mitch nodded solemnly. "How is he otherwise? Is he coping okay?"

"He wouldn't talk to me for almost a week," I told him. "He was so quiet, I thought for sure he was going to leave me."

Mitch frowned, but he looked at me concerned. "What happened?"

I exhaled loudly. "He kind of lost it the day before yesterday. He was so quiet, and he wouldn't talk to me, and he wouldn't eat, and he was so angry. It was just under the surface, ya know? Like it was right there, but he wouldn't talk about it no matter what I tried. Then I just said something totally unrelated and he lost it at me."

"Oh, man."

"Yeah, he yelled and screamed at me, then he was crying," I said quietly. "It was awful, but he needed it. He's been better since." Mitch just nodded, so I asked him, "How's Anna? I mean how is she really?"

"She can't sleep," he said. "She has bad nightmares. The doctor gave her pills to help her sleep at night, but she doesn't like taking them."

"Yeah, Kira doesn't sleep very well," I told him. "Sometimes he won't wake up, but he'll just toss and turn and mumble. Other times he'll wake up in a sweat, or he'll be clinging to me in his sleep."

Mitch nodded. "Yeah, Anna's much the same." Then he kind of smiled.

"What?"

"It's just weird to hear you talk about anyone like that," Mitch answered.

"Is it because he's a guy?" I asked, figuring when it was just me and him, he'd tell me his honest thoughts.

"No, it isn't," he said softly. "I told you before it doesn't bother me. It's just weird. I don't know. You've never talked about anyone... or dated anyone." Then he corrected, "Well, that I've known about anyway."

"No, I haven't dated anyone," I admitted. "I mean, there's been guys..." I trailed off, feeling my face heat with embarrassment. "It feels weird talking about this. I've never had anyone I could talk to about any of this, about Kira, about what he means to me."

Mitch looked at me for a long time. "That must have been hard for you."

"It was. But I never had anyone in my life for a long time. Not since my mom died. Kira's really the first."

"You've had me," he said kindly. "And the other guys."

"Yeah, I have," I conceded. "But it's not the same. I never realized what was missing until I found him."

"I'm sorry you could never tell me about any of that."

I sighed and looked out over the forest. "I love him," I said quietly. "I won't apologize for that. I've never had to come out before, and I don't know what that means for my job."

Mitch frowned. "I'm sure no one will care, given what we went through."

I shrugged. "Maybe. But that's not what I meant."

Mitch cocked one eyebrow at me. "What did you mean?"

"I don't know if I want my job," I said softly. "I don't know if I want to be a cop anymore."

Mitch looked at me, unblinking, stunned.

I looked out over the forest again, unable to look at him. "What happened to Kira was my fault," I said. "It wouldn't have happened if I wasn't a cop. I can't let anything happen to him again."

"Matt, no," Mitch said. "No. It's not your fault, it's not anyone's fault. Tomic was a sadistic bastard. What he did to the girls and to Frankie is his doing. Not anyone else's. You can't live with that type of guilt, Matt. It will eat you alive."

I shrugged again, hearing what he said, but not believing it. "You don't feel guilty for what happened to Anna?"

Mitch opened his mouth to say something, but quickly snapped it shut and looked out over the forest.

"Guilt is a natural emotional response to such a stressful situation," I quoted some spiel I'd heard a counselor say. Then I snorted. "What a fucking joke."

Mitch nodded. "What will you do?"

"I don't know," I told him. "I haven't decided."

"You need to talk to Kurt and Tony," he told me. "And Berkman."

"I will."

He nodded. "Will you tell me first, if you decide to quit? Matt, you're my partner. I trust you with my life. I don't trust anyone else like I trust you."

"You're not making it easier for me," I said with half a grin.

"I don't want you to leave," he said. "I can't stop you, if it's what you decide you really want. But I'd miss your sorry face."

I smiled. "Yeah, thanks."

"What does Frankie think?"

"I haven't told him," I admitted. "He doesn't need my guilt on top of his own."

"Hey!" Anna's voice called out from down on ground level. "You two ready for lunch? We're hungry."

We took the trail through the woods to the café. Anna and Kira walked in front of us, still with arms linked, talking quietly amongst themselves, while Mitch and I walked behind. "I think these two might be up to making mischief," Mitch said with a smile.

Anna looked over her shoulder at us and poked her tongue out at Mitch. "For that, you can buy lunch."

Mitch smiled lovingly at her, and when we got to the café and slid into a booth, Mitch was quick to put his arm around her. He kissed the side of her head and asked her quietly, "Do you feel okay? Not too tired?"

She shook her head and smiled in return. "Not at all. In fact, I feel much better."

"I do too," Kira added. "I've been worried about you and the others."

I rubbed my thumb on his back. "We can call them now if you want," I told him. "Or later this afternoon."

Kira smiled at me. "I think I'd like to go see them, actually." Then he added, as if he was unsure if I'd approve, "If that's okay..."

"Of course that's fine. I think that's a better idea, anyway. I really should talk to the guys," I said, looking at Mitch. "We have a lot to talk about."

Kira put his hand on my thigh. "We could see what they're doing tomorrow, if you want to head back to the city. Plus I really should see my parents. They've been asking when we're coming home."

I couldn't help but frown. "We can head back tomorrow," I told him. "Anyway, I guess I have to face your parents sometime. Can't put it off forever."

"Matt, baby," he said softly. "They don't blame you. No

one blames you. We've been through this. Please tell me you're okay with it."

Right then, our server interrupted us, saving me from answering. "You guys ready to order?"

I smiled at her. "Coffee, please."

FOUR WEEKS LATER

KIRA STARTED the grill as we brought in the last of the boxes. We'd done all the heavy furniture first, so this was the last of it. Mitch opened the fridge. "Who wants a beer?" he asked rhetorically.

We all fell into deck chairs on the patio and groaned.

"Next time you wanna move from an apartment on the seventh floor, hire a moving company," Kurt moaned.

Mitch brought out five Sams and handed us each one beer. "*I'll* pay for someone else to do it," he huffed. "My back is killing me."

Anna walked out to where we were with a bowl of salad in hand. "You sound like a bunch of old women."

Kira laughed. Given his arm was still in a cast, he hadn't been able to help us move much. He'd probably lifted more than he should have, but he was stubborn and proud. He was also the biggest and strongest out of all of us and found it hard to stand by and watch.

Although Chris was keen to keep him on at work at the gym, Kira was reduced to limited shifts with restricted duties with his injuries, which meant his income was limited. When he'd said he'd have to give up his apartment and find somewhere cheaper or move back in with his parents, I'd told him I knew of a place. "It's rent free, lots of space, there's even a yard."

He'd looked at me dubiously. "What's the catch?"

I'd nodded seriously. "You'd have to share a bedroom."

The look on his face had been priceless. I'd laughed. "Move in with me."

It had taken some discussion, some convincing. We'd only been together for a few months, after all. It was a huge step in our relationship, but it was just right for us. And in the end, he'd agreed and so that was what we did.

We'd moved his entire apartment down seven fucking flights of stairs.

So after over a decade, my house was finally becoming a home again. Kira was keen to repaint and do some minor renovations, but to be honest, I was just over the moon we'd be living together. Just me and him.

So as a thank you, Kira and I were putting on a cookout lunch. The women had been doing the inside, sorting out boxes and setting up house. They adored Kira; they doted on him. Mitch, Kurt, and Tony had accepted him completely.

When we'd left the cabin the day after Mitch and Anna visited, we'd stopped in to see them. Kurt and Rachel first, then Tony and Evie.

Kurt was fine with it, more concerned after not hearing from me for over a week. But Rachel had hugged Kira, and like Anna, had cried when she first saw him. I asked Kurt outright if he had any problems with me being gay, and he swore he didn't. When I asked him if he had doubts about being a cop, he took a second to answer. Then he sighed. "I've thought about it," he admitted. "But it's what we do, right? If Rachel wanted me to quit, then I would, but she said she's okay with it." Then he studied me. "Are you having doubts?"

I nodded. "I just don't know."

"Maybe you just need some time," he said.

"Yeah, maybe," was about all I could answer.

I was nervous about seeing Tony. When the whole Tomic ordeal was going down, he'd been the one who called me a fag. And funnily enough, when we arrived at his house, it was the first thing he apologized for. He said he was stressed, like everyone else, but there was no real excuse for such a horrible thing to say.

Evie didn't cry when she first saw Kira. She just kept trying to feed him. She told him it was the Italian in her that prompted her to feed and care for her boys. It was only when Kira admitted to not much of an appetite since the ordeal that Evie's eyes welled with tears.

She thanked him a dozen times over for everything he went through. "That man grabbed me and you stopped him," she said through her tears. "I'll never thank you enough."

It was then Tony got teary himself. "Same goes for me, Frankie. Forever indebted to you."

Kira just shrugged modestly. "Any one of you guys would have done the same thing."

Tony shook his head in wonder, then looked at me. "He's a real good guy, Matt."

I smiled warmly at him. "I know."

Maybe me being gay would have been an issue the guys couldn't get past, if it weren't for Kira being the hero and saving their partners. Kira and Anna had grown particularly close. In fact, Kira had bonded with Anna, Rachel, and Evie over their ordeal, and so by association, Mitch, Kurt, and

Tony had gotten to know him too. More than their initial gratitude, they'd gotten to *know* him. The more they saw him, and saw us together, the more they got to see the real him. The generous, smart and funny guy I fell in love with.

It wasn't all easy. They all said they understood why I'd lived a closeted life, though I think it was the respect and admiration for Kira and what he did for them that made it easier for the guys to accept. That, and the fact Anna, Rachel, and Evie would tear them all a new one if they didn't deal with it.

I called Berkman to let him know we were back in town, and he was quick to visit. He was concerned for Kira, of course, and checking he was okay—and reinforcing his offer of department-provided counseling. Kira gave us some time alone.

I told Berkman outright I wasn't sure if I wanted to be a cop anymore. He ran his hands through his hair a few times and the wrinkles at his eyes deepened. "What do the others think?" he asked.

"They want me to stay," I told him. "They said they can't make that decision for me."

"And what does Kira think?"

"I haven't mentioned it," I admitted. "He's got enough on his plate right now."

Berkman exhaled through puffed cheeks. "Well, Elliott, you know what I think you need?"

"No."

"I think you need to get back on the job. Normally I'd say take all the time you need, but you're a cop through and through, Elliott. You don't know how to be anything else. Maybe the routine and familiarity will do you good." Then he added, "I'll get you scheduled to see the counselor along with everyone else."

"Ross..."

"Don't argue with me, son."

I rolled my eyes, but then I smiled. "What do you want me to do?"

"I want you to come into HQ during the week," he said. "Line it up with the other guys for a mid-week meeting, and we'll talk it out."

So that was what we did. I still wasn't sure if I was doing the right thing. My head certainly wasn't in the right place, but I thought maybe Berkman was right. Maybe with a bit of time doing familiar things with a familiar routine would put me back on track.

And for the most part, work was much the same. The whole ordeal had been a strain on everyone, as individuals, as couples, as cops. And not just us, but the other cops as well.

Most of them gave us space and pats on the back, and the fact that I'd come out as gay didn't make too many waves. There was only once, when one asshole made one passing "fag" comment. I'd stopped and turned to give this guy a piece of my mind, but I didn't have to. Because Mitch, Kurt, and Tony stood in front of me, and it was Tony who let him have it. Needless to say, no one had said anything since. They defended Kira like he was one of us.

So when we needed to move Kira's stuff from his place to mine, the guys didn't hesitate to help. Though I'd bet money they'd regret it tomorrow—the four of us were aching already.

After we'd eaten lunch, we were sitting around enjoying the afternoon sun, talking crap like we always did, when there was a knock at the door. Kira got up to get to see who it was, and he walked out with an unexpected guest.

Berkman.

Our boss had been rather patient with me, all things considered. At some point I decided my part of the Fab Four was worth something, and we agreed the four of us would stay as a team. Berkman never pressured us. Sure, he gave us orders and put us back to work soon enough, but he also gave us space and time, and everything the department had to offer. The more I thought about it, the more I wondered if the lack of gay comments from the other cops had something to do with Berkman threatening bodily harm.

"Hey, thanks for the invite," he said sarcastically, sitting himself at the table, swiping my beer. He took a mouthful and sighed while we waited for him to explain the reason for his visit.

Berkman knew we were moving Kira into my house today, so he knew where to find us all in one place. He sighed again. "The DA's office called me about an hour ago," he said seriously. "Pavao Tomic was found dead in his cell this morning."

Everyone blinked. No one said a word. Kira got up, walked back inside and came out with a fresh beer for me.

"He's supposed to be in court tomorrow," Tony said out loud.

"Well, not any more, he's not," Kurt replied.

"Goddammit," Mitch huffed.

It was a hollow closure, somewhat dissatisfying. We all knew it. We all felt the same.

"So what does that mean for the Tomic case?" Kira asked.

I shrugged. "It's over. We can still pursue Tomic's men, but as for the Tomic twins, it's case closed."

"Just like that?"

I nodded. "Just like that."

Mitch sighed. "So what do we do tomorrow?"

"New cases, new bad guys," Berkman said simply. He looked around the table at us, held up his beer, and we all clinked our bottles to his.

I didn't know if I was doing the right thing or not, but I looked around at the others sitting at the table, and smiled at the faces looking back at me. "To new cases, new bad guys."

~ THE END

It was a usual Friday night at the bar. Except it wasn't.

My partners Mitch, Kurt, and Tony were there with me. My boyfriend Kira was there too, along with my boss, Berkman, and most of the guys from my division. There were celebratory drinks, a tab on the bar, and congratulations all round.

I should have been happy. And part of me was. But part of me wasn't. The smile on my face and laughs with the boys didn't quite sit right, but the more I had to drink, the easier it got.

"Here it is!" someone called out. "Turn it up!"

The attention in the bar was drawn to the TV as the bartender turned up the volume.

"... in this breaking story, after almost eleven years, Detective Matthew Elliott has announced his resignation from the LAPD..."

There were cheers and applause from around the bar, a few claps on my shoulder. Kira squeezed my thigh under the table. I smiled and lifted my beer in a salute before taking another swig.

I hated press conferences. I had a healthy distaste for the media and the paparazzi and I hated having to put my life on display for the public. Yet there I stood in front of a dozen cameras and even more reporters about to give the biggest announcement of my career.

It was ironic that the biggest would be my last.

I was on screen announcing to the good people, and the not-so good people, of LA that I was no longer a detective. I was no longer a part of the Fab Four. I was no longer a cop.

The questions started, and I heard myself reel off the well-rehearsed answers on the TV. I'd given dozens of press conferences over my time with the LAPD Narcotics Division, and I'd never dreamed I'd be standing there announcing to the world that I was walking away from all I'd ever known.

Yet there I was, doing exactly that.

The questions on screen continued.

"Can you tell us why? Why are you retiring, Detective Elliott?" one reporter asked.

"Does this have anything to do with being outed as a gay cop last year?"

"Where does this leave the Fab Four? Do you have a replacement?"

"Are you planning a career in politics?"

I laughed at that, on screen and at the table in the bar. Mitch, who was sitting across from me, laughed as well. "No plans for running for governor? Come on," Mitch joked. "You'd make a good politician."

I finished the last mouthful of my beer and pointed my empty bottle at him. Instead of telling him to get fucked, I said, "My turn to buy. 'Nother beer?"

"Hell yes, if you're payin'," he slurred.

I turned to Kira and leaned in toward him and asked,

"Drink, baby?" He shook his head at me. I must've been drunk if I'd called him "baby" in front of the boys. Fuck.

"Nah, I'm fine," he said. "Someone has to make sure you get home okay."

"'M sorry," I said, trying to apologize. "'S been a big day."

Kira smiled sadly. "I know it has."

I nodded and stood up off my stool. I swayed as I made my way to the bar. I was drunk. It had been an emotional day, after an emotionally charged few weeks since I'd announced that I was leaving.

It hadn't been easy. It had been one of the hardest decisions I'd ever made, but it was the right decision. My partners at work, Mitch, Kurt, and Tony, were surprisingly okay with it. My boss had warned me against it, but ultimately agreed it was the right thing, but Kira... Kira didn't like the idea at all.

He didn't understand why I was leaving the department. No matter what reason I gave him, he didn't believe me. He knew I loved my job, it was a part of who I was, he'd said.

And it had been a bone of contention between us since.

It wasn't that he wasn't being supportive. He just didn't understand. I told him it was a decision I'd toyed with over the last twelve months, since he was abducted and tortured, beaten, held hostage because of me. And that wasn't a lie. It just wasn't the whole truth.

The whole truth was something I couldn't tell him.

Kira knew there was something else to it. Of course he did. We'd been living together for almost twelve months, he *knew* me. And I'd never lied to him before. I'd never had to. And he knew I wasn't telling him something.

He'd get quiet whenever I talked about leaving, waiting

for me to explain the truth, but I never did. The night I told him I'd handed in my resignation was our first real fight. He yelled and I yelled back, and he threw a glass into the sink and I slammed some doors.

We hadn't spoken for two days afterwards.

It had damn near killed me.

A hard thump on my arm and a large hand on my shoulder snapped me out of my memories. My boss, my ex-boss, Berkman stood beside me and threw some twenties on the bar. "Whatever this man wants," he told the barman.

I ordered some shots of bourbon under the watchful eye of the man who'd been like a father to me. I looked at him and gave him the best confident smile I could fake.

"You sure about this?" he asked quietly.

I nodded. "Yeah..."

The older man's jaw bulged and he exhaled through his nose. "But?"

I looked back to where Kira was sitting with Mitch and the others. "I've never lied to him," I said, suddenly feeling every drink I'd had.

Berkman nodded. "It won't be easy."

"Mmm," I agreed, swaying where I stood. I didn't want to talk about it. Not here, anyway. Not that Berkman would have said anything. "Need another drink," I mumbled, picking up a fresh shot of liquor. I threw back the bourbon and when I put the glass back down, the bar wasn't as close as I thought. Berkman put his hands on me, I realized, to steady me. Fuck, I was drunk.

"I'll carry these to the table," Berkman said, indicating to the drinks on the bar. Then he faced me in the direction of where Kira and Mitch were sitting. "You go that way."

The bar was loud and busy and as I crossed the floor, I bumped into familiar faces with pats on the back and rounds of good luck and best wishes. Berkman beat me back to the table with my drinks, and when I finally got there, everyone was smiling at me.

I slid my arm around Kira's shoulder, and he maneuvered me onto my stool and handed me a drink. I held up the single shot, and Mitch, Kurt, Tony, and Berkman all raised theirs. Kira held up his soda, and they all bumped their glasses against mine.

"To Matt," Berkman declared. "To the future and wherever it may take you. We wish you well."

"Cheers!"

"To Matt!"

I downed my shot and sucked back the afterburn. "Fuck. I'm gonna be sick tomorrow."

"And you don't have to be in the office by eight!" Kurt cried. He looked as drunk as I felt. "You get to sleep in!"

I laughed. "No more all-nighters, no more double shifts. I am done with that shit."

Mitch shook his head at me. "You really doin' it," he slurred. "You really won't be there tomorrow?"

I shook my head. "Nope."

"Fuck," Mitch mumbled. He pointed his finger at me. "If I get some rookie punk as a partner, I'm gonna kick your ass."

I laughed at him. "Like to see ya try."

He shook his head at me. "You really gonna do that fighting thing?"

I grinned and raised my hands to protect my chin. "Yep."

"You're fucking crazy," Mitch said, shaking his head.

"Yeah, maybe that's why he left," Kurt said with a sly grin. "Hey, Berkman," he called out to the boss. "Did Elliot fail his psych?"

The older man snorted. "You *all* failed psych."

Everyone laughed, and even Kira smiled and shook his head at us.

"So when do you start?" Tony asked. I was pretty sure I'd told them all this already. "This new career of yours."

"Monday," I answered. "I plan on being very sick tomorrow and possibly still sick on Sunday, but I'm signed up for first official session on Monday."

"You know," Mitch said thoughtfully. "If you want to pay good money to get beaten up, you could've just paid me."

"Fucking boxing," Kurt said, shaking his head.

"It's not boxing," I corrected him, for the twentieth time. "It's MMA."

"Mixed martial arts, what-the-fuck-ever," he said, rolling his eyes. "It's punishment, that's what it is."

"Frankie." Tony called Kira by his nickname. Most of the guys still did. "Frankie, talk some sense into this boy."

"I've tried," Kira said quietly, turning his glass of soda on the table. "I thought you guys might have had more luck. He won't listen to me."

I sighed. "We're not going through this again. It's a done deal," I told them. "Cheer up, boys. It's my farewell." I changed the topic. "Whose turn is it to buy me a drink?"

It was all an act.

We each had our part.

Everyone at that table had a role to play. Except Kira.

And that was what tore at me. That was what made this so damn hard.

I'd been part of covert ops before. I'd done my time undercover. That was until our little group of the famous Fab Four had our faces plastered on every screen, newspaper, and internet news and celebrity site. Any chances of us doing undercover work again were pretty much over.

Unless one of us wasn't a cop anymore.

If one of us left the police, left the spotlight, left everything we'd ever known, then maybe one of us could get some inside information on a drug ring we'd been watching for months.

It would have to be public. It would have to be completely watertight, and it would have to be, for all intents and purposes, very real.

No one would know.

No one would know I was going undercover, except Mitch, Kurt, Tony, and Berkman.

Not even Kira.

For his own safety, he could have no part in this.

Kira knew my decision to leave my job hadn't been easy for me, he just didn't understand why. I'd told him I'd had enough. The last twelve months since his abduction and beating had been hard—not just for him, not just for me, but for everyone. I told him I realized while I loved my job, I loved him more ,and I would never risk his safety again.

And as much as that was true, I couldn't tell him the whole truth.

He disputed the whole idea and God, we argued. But at the end of the day, I had a job to do.

I didn't know what this would mean for us. I didn't know where it would lead or how long it would take. Months, a year... there was no way of knowing.

I loved him, and I knew he loved me. I just hoped it would be enough.

I looked at him and squeezed his thigh. I'd had far too much to drink, and I really needed to go home. Even drunk, a part of me didn't want the night to end. Because I knew, when I woke up in the morning, not only was I going to be hungover, I was also going to be *just* Matt Elliot. Not a cop, not a detective. And I didn't know what it was like to not have that security, that camaraderie. My brothers.

That was what it felt like.

It felt like I was losing my brothers.

"Love you guys," I told them.

"Oh, fuck," Mitch said, standing up. "He's up to the 'I love yous.' That's Matthew Elliott code for 'I'm drunk.' It's time to get him home."

"Don't be like that," I said, shaking my head. I knew I was drunk. I knew my words were slurred and I was not staying upright very well, but I knew what tonight meant.

"You's are my family, my brothers," I told them, suddenly choking up on emotion. "I'm gonna miss ya's." I looked at Mitch. "You the most, you son of a bitch."

He smiled and said something I think was supposed to be funny, but when he hugged me, he hugged me hard. He whispered in my ear, "I'll miss you too."

Kira was standing beside me now, and Mitch handed me over to him. "Get him home," he said. Mitch looked a little teary-eyed, and he smiled sadly. "Jesus Christ, Elliott. Never would have thought I'd be sorry to see the back of ya."

I had more claps on the back, another round of applause from the cops who were still there, and they dragged my sorry ass out the door. I hugged Tony and Kurt, and even Berkman, who handed me back to Kira. Apparently to keep me upright. I told them all I loved them again, then I told them leaving the police department wasn't as hard as it was to say goodbye to them.

"It's not really goodbye," Kurt said kindly. "You'll see us all the time. We'll do barbeques and poker or something."

"Yeah, dinner with me and Anna next weekend, remember?" Mitch said. "Jesus, don't forget that, or she'll kill me."

Tony hugged me. "Yeah, and you'll see us laughing as we write you up for parking tickets, traffic violations, jaywalking..."

They all laughed, but I frowned. "'S not funny."

"Yes it is," they said in unison, and with another round of laughter and goodbyes, they bundled me into Kira's car. They stood on the sidewalk as we pulled out onto the street, and it was weird. As drunk as I was, I knew the look on their faces would stay with me.

My head fell back on the headrest, and I exhaled loudly. "Gonna miss them."

Kira was quiet for a long while, and I turned my head to look at him. He looked at me, then back to the road as he drove. "Then why are you leaving?"

I sighed, and the last shot of bourbon swirled through my brain. "You know why. I've told you why." I was drunk and was sick of having this conversation with him, and my words probably sounded harsher than I meant them to.

He shook his head. "Whatever."

Whatever. He fucking said "whatever" to me. Well, fuck that shit. Deciding I needed fresh air right the fuck now, I tried to wind down the window, but the little button wouldn't work. "What the fuck is wrong with your window?"

"Nothing," he answered calmly. "It was locked." Then he pressed a button and all of a sudden my window went down.

I sighed. "Whatever."

The rest of the car trip home was quiet, and when we pulled up in the drive, he opened my door and offered to help me out of the car. "I can get out myself," I snapped at him, then almost fell out of the car. I lined up the front steps and stumbled toward them. "I don't need your help," I told him, so he left me, walked up the front steps, and opened the door. And those front steps looked a mile high. "Babe?" I called out, feeling myself sway and stagger. Kira stopped and turned back to face me. "I need your help."

He tried not to smile as he came back down the steps toward me. "Thought you said you didn't need me."

"I do need you."

He grabbed me as I misstepped. "I can see that."

"Sorry I'm drunk," I told him.

"It's okay."

"Sorry 'bout before."

He helped me up the steps. "It's okay, Matt."

"Sorry, babe," I apologized again. "Sorry I love you."

He hauled me inside and shut the front door behind us. He stopped walking and held me up so he could look in my eyes. "Don't apologize for that," he said.

I put my hand to the side of his face. "I'm drunk."

"I know."

"I'm sorry."

"I know."

He slung his arm around me and led me to our room. I just wanted to lie down, but he kept me upright and pulled my shirt off.

"Love you," I told him.

"I know."

I swayed and Kira steadied me. "I'm really drunk."

"I know." He undid my jeans and pushed them over my hips.

"Too drunk for sex, babe," I told him.

He laughed. "I know."

I fell onto the bed and Kira pulled my boots off, then my jeans. The room started to spin and not even closing my eyes made it stop. I groaned. "Love you."

I felt his lips at my temple. "I know."

For more of N.R. Walker's books, including Breaking Point and Starting Point, visit her Amazon Page

ABOUT THE AUTHOR

N.R. Walker is an Australian author, who loves her genre of gay romance. She loves writing and spends far too much time doing it, but wouldn't have it any other way.

She is many things: a mother, a wife, a sister, a writer. She has pretty, pretty boys who live in her head, who don't let her sleep at night unless she gives them life with words. She likes it when they do dirty, dirty things... but likes it even more when they fall in love.

She used to think having people in her head talking to her was weird, until one day she happened across other writers who told her it was normal.

She's been writing ever since...

CONTACT N.R. WALKER

Website

Facebook

Facebook Author Page

Twitter

Instagram

Amazon Page

Google +

Email:
nrwalker@nrwalker.net

The Spencer Cohen Series, Book One

The Spencer Cohen Series, Book Two

The Spencer Cohen Series, Book Three

The Spencer Cohen Series, Yanni's Story

Blood & Milk

The Weight Of It All

A Very Henry Christmas (The Weight of It All 1.5)

Perfect Catch

Switched

Imago

Imagines

Red Dirt Heart Imago

On Davis Row

Finders Keepers

Evolved

Galaxies and Oceans

Private Charter

Nova Praetorian

Titles in Audio:

Cronin's Key

Cronin's Key II

Cronin's Key III

Red Dirt Heart

Red Dirt Heart 2

Red Dirt Heart 3

Red Dirt Heart 4

The Weight Of It All

Switched

Point of No Return

Breaking Point

Starting Point

Spencer Cohen Book One

Spencer Cohen Book Two

Spencer Cohen Book Three

Yanni's Story

On Davis Row

Evolved

Free Reads:

Sixty Five Hours

Learning to Feel

His Grandfather's Watch (And The Story of Billy and Hale)

The Twelfth of Never (Blind Faith 3.5)

Twelve Days of Christmas (Sixty Five Hours Christmas)

Best of Both Worlds

Translated Titles:

Fiducia Cieca (Italian translation of Blind Faith)

Attraverso Questi Occhi (Italian translation of Through These Eyes)

Preso alla Sprovvista (Italian translation of Blindside)

Il giorno del Mai (Italian translation of Blind Faith 3.5)

Cuore di Terra Rossa (Italian translation of Red Dirt Heart)

Cuore di Terra Rossa 2 (Italian translation of Red Dirt Heart 2)

Cuore di Terra Rossa 3 (Italian translation of Red Dirt Heart 3)

Cuore di Terra Rossa 4 (Italian translation of Red Dirt Heart 4)

Intervento di Retrofit (Italian translation of Elements of Retrofit)

Confiance Aveugle (French translation of Blind Faith)

A travers ces yeux: Confiance Aveugle 2 (French translation of Through These Eyes)

Aveugle: Confiance Aveugle 3 (French translation of Blindside)

À Jamais (French translation of Blind Faith 3.5)

Cronin's Key (French translation)

Cronin's Key II (French translation)

Au Coeur de Sutton Station (French translation of Red Dirt Heart)

Partir ou rester (French translation of Red Dirt Heart 2)

Faire Face (French translation of Red Dirt Heart 3)

Trouver sa Place (French translation of Red Dirt Heart 4)

Rote Erde (German translation of Red Dirt Heart)

Rote Erde 2 (German translation of Red Dirt Heart 2)

9 781925 886245